Selected Stories by
HOWARD PYLE

Books in this Series:

Selected Stories by O. Henry
Selected Stories by Anton Chekhov
Selected Stories by Guy de Maupassant
Selected Stories by Mark Twain
Selected Stories by Edgar Allan Poe
Selected Stories by Rudyard Kipling
Selected Stories by Saki
Selected Stories by Oscar Wilde
Selected Stories by Honoré de Balzac
Selected Stories by Charles Dickens
Selected Stories by D.H. Lawrence
Selected Stories by H.G. Wells
Selected Stories by Jack London
Selected Stories by Joseph Conrad
Selected Stories by Leo Tolstoy
Selected Stories by Sir Arthur Conan Doyle
Selected Stories by James Joyce
Selected Stories by Virginia Woolf
Selected Stories by Thomas Hardy
Selected Stories by Fyodor Dostoyevsky
Selected Stories by Katherine Mansfield
Selected Stories by Wilkie Collins
Selected Stories by Robert Louis Stevenson

Selected Stories by
HOWARD PYLE

RUPA

Published by
Rupa Publications India Pvt. Ltd 2014
7/16, Ansari Road, Daryaganj
New Delhi 110002

Sales Centres:
Allahabad Bengaluru Chennai
Hyderabad Jaipur Kathmandu
Kolkata Mumbai

Selection and Introduction copyright © Terry O'Brien 2014

All rights reserved.
No part of this publication may be reproduced, transmitted,
or stored in a retrieval system, in any form or by any means,
electronic, mechanical, photocopying, recording or otherwise,
without the prior permission of the publisher.

ISBN: 978-81-291-3526-1

First impression 2014

10 9 8 7 6 5 4 3 2 1

Printed at Shree Maitrey Printech Pvt. Ltd., Noida

This book is sold subject to the condition that it shall not,
by way of trade or otherwise, be lent, resold, hired out, or otherwise
circulated, without the publisher's prior consent, in any form of binding or
cover other than that in which it is published.

CONTENTS

Introduction vii

1. All Things are as Fate Wills 1
2. Claus and his Wonderful Staff 11
3. Clever Peter and the Two Bottles 20
4. The Enchanted Island 30
5. Empty Bottles 43
6. The Fruit of Happiness 51
7. Ill-Luck and the Fiddler 63
8. Little Snowdrop 72
9. Not a Pin to Choose 82
10. A Piece of Good Luck 101
11. The Salt of Life 121
12. Woman's Wit 137

INTRODUCTION

Howard Pyle (5 March 1853–9 November 1911) was an American illustrator and author, primarily of books for young people. In 1894, he began teaching illustration at the Drexel Institute of Art, Science and Industry (now Drexel University). After 1900, he founded his own school of art and illustration, named the Howard Pyle School of Illustration Art. His 1883 classic publication *The Merry Adventures of Robin Hood* remains in print, and his other books, frequently with medieval European settings, include a four-volume set on *King Arthur*. He is also well known for his illustrations of pirates, and is credited with creating what has become the modern stereotype of pirate dress.

These stories have been handpicked from *The Twilight* and *Salt and Pepper*, which he especially wrote for his nine-year-old daughter Phoebe.

- 'All Things are as Fate Wills' is an enchanting fairy tale which begins with a wise king having these exact words placed all over his palace, for he truly believes that it is fate which controls man. His son, the successor, however, refuses to abide by them and is determined to prove instead that 'all things are as man does'.
- 'Claus and his Wonderful Staff' is the story of two brothers, Hans the rich brother and Claus the poor one.

The story reveals how Claus goes out into the world with his wonderful staff to find his own fortune, and indeed comes upon something magnificent.
- In the story 'Clever Peter and the Two Bottles', Peter is thought to be a fool by everyone but his mother. He eventually proves his mother right, however, when one morning he goes out to sell eggs and on the way meets a mysterious old stranger with whom he strikes an extraordinary bargain.
- 'The Enchanted Island' is a fantastic tale with a real message, that of true wisdom trumping fickle luck. The story revolves around Selim the Baker and Selim the Fisherman, the former of which chooses to wear the Ring of Luck, leaving the latter to don the Ring of Wisdom. As the story continues, it becomes evident which is the better choice.
- 'Empty Bottles' is a story that revolves around the interaction between a great magician and physician, by the name of Nicholas Flamel and a student named Gebhart, who could patter off everything he had learned in books. The student goes to the wise old man to be taught by him, and the latter puts him to a rather biting test.
- 'The Fruit of Happiness' revolves around a servant who, after having served a wise man for seven long years, decides to go out into the world and make his own fortune. On his way, he meets an angel in the guise of a common traveller and comes to see fantastic happenings.
- 'Ill-Luck and the Fiddler' is the story of how a Fiddler comes across Ill-Luck on his travels, and is persuaded by the latter to take him along with him. Eventually the Fiddler comes across a rich man and later, a queen, both of which favourable encounters are foiled by Ill-Luck in the most extraordinary ways.

- 'Little Snowdrop' is the story of a beautiful little princess called Snowdrop who is envied by her evil stepmother for her beauty. The latter makes several attempts to kill her, just so she may reign as the fairest of all.
- The tale 'Not a Pin to Choose' begins with a fagot-maker, Abdallah, bemoaning the fact that he has been duped out of his money by his friend Ali, whom he had helped and trusted so much. A wise man preaches to him of how no man ever loves someone who is always giving, but Abdallah claims that he would always be grateful in such a scenario. The veracity of that claim is questioned through the plot of the story.
- 'A Piece of Good Luck' begins with three students who, on the completion of their studies, are given three glass balls by their master, each of which, on dropping to the ground, would yield treasure. While two of the trio discover gold and silver, the third discovers a piece of good luck.
- In 'The Salt of Life', a king who had three sons asks each of them how much they love him. While the older two answer that they love him as much as gold and silver, the youngest replies that he loves him as much as salt. The answer angers the king who turns him out, but eventually it is this answer which is proved the most truthful in the end.
- 'Woman's Wit' is the story of how a naive tailor is caught in the trap of a demon and can devise no way to get rid of him. It is eventually his wife, the princess, who manages to best the demon with her wit.

1

ALL THINGS ARE AS FATE WILLS

Once upon a time, in the old, old days, there lived a king who had a head upon his shoulders wiser than other folk, and this was why: though he was richer and wiser and greater than most kings, and had all that he wanted and more into the bargain, he was so afraid of becoming proud of his own prosperity that he had these words written in letters of gold upon the walls of each and every room in his palace:

All Things are as Fate wills.

Now, by and by and after a while, the king died; for when his time comes, even the rich and the wise man must die, as well as the poor and the simple man. So the king's son came, in turn, to be king of that land; and, though he was not so bad as the world of men goes, he was not the man that his father was, as this story will show you.

One day, as he sat with his chief councillor, his eyes fell upon the words written in letters of gold upon the wall—the words that his father had written there in time gone by:

All Things are as Fate wills; and the young king did not like the taste of them, for he was very proud of his own greatness. 'That is not so,' said he, pointing to the words on the wall. 'Let them be painted out, and these words written in their place:

All Things are as Man does.'

Now, the chief councillor was a grave old man, and had been councillor to the young king's father. 'Do not be too hasty, my lord king,' said he. 'Try first the truth of your own words before you wipe out those that your father has written.'

'Very well,' said the young king, 'so be it. I will approve the truth of my words. Bring me hither some beggar from the town whom Fate has made poor, and I will make him rich. So I will show you that his life shall be as I will, and not as Fate wills.'

Now, in that town there was a poor beggar-man who used to sit every day beside the town gate, begging for something for charity's sake. Sometimes people gave him a penny or two, but it was little or nothing that he got, for Fate was against him.

The same day that the king and the chief councillor had had their talk together, as the beggar sat holding up his wooden bowl and asking charity of those who passed by, there suddenly came three men who, without saying a word, clapped hold of him and marched him off.

It was in vain that the beggar talked and questioned—in vain that he begged and besought them to let him go. Not a word did they say to him, either of good or bad. At last they came to a gate that led through a high wall and into a garden, and there the three stopped, and one of them knocked upon the gate. In answer to his knocking it flew open. He thrust the beggar into the garden neck and crop, and then the gate was banged to again.

But what a sight it was the beggar saw before his eyes!— flowers, and fruit trees, and marble walks, and a great fountain that shot up a jet of water as white as snow. But he had not long to stand gaping and staring around him, for in the garden were a great number of people, who came hurrying to him, and who, without speaking a word to him or answering a single question, or as much as giving him time to think, led him to a marble bath of tepid water. There he was stripped of his tattered clothes and washed as clean as snow. Then, as some of the attendants dried him with fine linen towels, others came carrying clothes fit for a prince to wear, and clad the beggar in them from head to foot. After that, still without saying a word, they let him out from the bath again, and there he found still other attendants waiting for him—two of them holding a milk-white horse, saddled and bridled, and fit for an emperor to ride. These helped him to mount, and then, leaping into their own saddles, rode away with the beggar in their midst.

They rode of the garden and into the streets, and on and on they went until they came to the king's palace, and there they stopped. Courtiers and noblemen and great lords were waiting for their coming, some of whom helped him to dismount from the horse, for by this time the beggar was so overcome with wonder that he stared like one moonstruck, and as though his wits were addled. Then, leading the way up the palace steps, they conducted him from room to room, until at last they came to one more grand and splendid than all the rest, and there sat the king himself waiting for the beggar's coming.

The beggar would have flung himself at the king's feet, but the king would not let him; for he came down from the throne where he sat, and, taking the beggar by the hand, led him up and sat him alongside of him. Then the king gave orders to the attendants who stood about, and a feast was served in plates of solid gold upon a tablecloth of silver—a feast such as the beggar had never dreamed of, and the poor man ate as he had never eaten in his life before.

All the while that the king and the beggar were eating, musicians played sweet music and dancers danced and singers sang.

Then, when the feast was over, there came ten young men, bringing flasks and flagons of all kinds, full of the best wine in the world; and the beggar drank as he had never drank in his life before, and until his head spun like a top.

So the king and the beggar feasted and made merry, until at last the clock struck twelve and the king arose from his seat. 'My friend,' said he to the beggar, 'all these things have been done to show you that Luck and Fate, which have been against you for all these years, are now for you. Hereafter, instead of being poor you shall be the richest of the rich, for I will give you the greatest thing that I have in my treasury.' Then he called the chief treasurer, who came forward with a golden tray in his hand. Upon the tray was a purse of silk. 'See,' said the king, 'here is a purse, and in the purse are one hundred pieces of gold money. But though that much may seem great to you, it is but little of the true value of the purse. Its virtue lies in this: that however much you may take from it, there will always be one hundred pieces of gold money left in it. Now go; and while you are enjoying the riches which I give you, I have only to ask you to remember these are not the gifts of Fate, but of a mortal man.'

But all the while he was talking the beggar's head was spinning and spinning, and buzzing and buzzing, so that he hardly heard a word of what the king said.

Then when the king had ended his speech, the lords and gentlemen who had brought the beggar in led him forth again. Out they went through room after room—out through the courtyard, out through the gate.

Bang!—it was shut to behind him, and he found himself standing in the darkness of midnight, with the splendid clothes upon his back, and the magic purse with its hundred pieces of gold money in his pocket.

He stood looking about himself for a while, and then off he started homeward, staggering and stumbling and shuffling, for the wine that he had drank made him so light-headed that all the world spun topsy-turvy around him.

His way led along by the river, and on he went stumbling and staggering. All of a sudden—plump! splash!—he was in the water over head and ears. Up he came, spitting out the water and shouting for help, splashing and sputtering, and kicking and swimming, knowing no more where he was than the man in the moon. Sometimes his head was under water and sometimes it was up again.

At last, just as his strength was failing him, his feet struck the bottom, and he crawled up on the shore more dead than alive. Then, through fear and cold and wet, he swooned away, and lay for a long time for all the world as though he were dead.

Now, it chanced that two fisherman were out with their nets that night, and Luck or Fate led them by the way where the beggar lay on the shore. 'Halloa!' said one of the fishermen, 'here is a poor body drowned!' They turned him over, and then they saw what rich clothes he wore, and felt that he had a purse in his pocket.

'Come,' said the second fisherman, 'he is dead, whoever he is. His fine clothes and his purse of money can do him no good now, and we might as well have them as anybody else.' So between them both they stripped the beggar of all that the king had given him, and left him lying on the beach.

At daybreak the beggar awoke from the swoon, and there he found himself lying without a stitch to his back, and half dead with the cold and the water he had swallowed. Then, fearing lest somebody might see him, he crawled away into the rushes that grew beside the river, there to hide himself until night should come again.

But as he went, crawling upon hands and knees, he suddenly came upon a bundle that had been washed up by the water, and when he laid eyes upon it his heart leaped within him, for what should that bundle be but the patches and tatters which he had worn the day before, and which the attendants had thrown over the garden wall and into the river when they had dressed him in the fine clothes the king gave him.

He spread his clothes out in the sun until they were dry, and then he put them on and went back into the town again.

'Well,' said the king, that morning, to his chief councillor, 'what do you think now? Am I not greater than Fate? Did I not make the beggar rich? And shall I not paint my father's words out from the wall, and put my own there instead?'

'I do not know,' said the councillor, shaking his head. 'Let us first see what has become of the beggar.'

'So be it,' said the king; and he and the councillor set off to see whether the beggar had done as he ought to do with the good things that the king had given him. So they came to the town gate, and there, lo and behold! The first thing that they saw was the beggar with his wooden bowl in his hand asking those who passed by for a stray penny or two.

When the king saw him he turned without a word, and rode back home again. 'Very well,' said he to the chief councillor, 'I have tried to make the beggar rich and have failed; nevertheless, if I cannot make him I can ruin him in spite of Fate, and that I will show you.'

So all that while the beggar sat at the town gate and begged until came noontide, when who should he see coming but the same three men who had come for him the day before. 'Ah, ha!' said he to himself, 'now the king is going to give me some more good things.' And so when the three reached him he was willing enough to go with them, rough as they were.

Off they marched; but this time they did not come to any garden with fruits and flowers and fountains and marble baths. Off they marched, and when they stopped it was in front of the king's palace. This time no nobles and great lords and courtiers were waiting for his coming; but instead of that the town hangman—a great ugly fellow, clad in black from head to foot. Up he came to the beggar, and, catching him by the scruff of his neck, dragged him up the palace steps and from room to room until at last he flung him down at the king's feet.

When the poor beggar gathered wits enough to look about him he saw there a great chest standing wide open, and with holes in the lid. He wondered what it was for, but the king gave him no chance to ask; for, beckoning with his hand, the hangman and the others caught the beggar by arms and legs, thrust him into the chest, and banged down the lid upon him.

The king locked it and double-locked it, and set his seal upon it; and there was the beggar as tight as a fly in a bottle.

They carried the chest out and thrust it into a cart and hauled it away, until at last they came to the sea shore. There they flung chest and all into the water, and it floated away like a cork. And that is how the king set about to ruin the poor beggar-man.

Well, the chest floated on and on for three days, and then at last it came to the shore of a country far away. There the waves caught it up, and flung it so hard upon the rocks of the sea beach that the chest was burst open by the blow, and the beggar crawled out with eyes as big as saucers and face as white as dough. After he had sat for a while, and when his wits came back to him and he had gathered strength enough, he stood up and looked around to see where Fate had cast him; and far away on the hillsides he saw the walls and the roofs and the towers of the great town, shining in the sunlight as white as snow.

'Well,' said he, 'here is something to be thankful for, at least,' and so saying and shaking the stiffness out of his knees and elbows, he started off for the white walls and the red roofs in the distance.

At last he reached the great gate, and through it he could see the stony streets and multitudes of people coming and going.

But it was not for him to enter that gate. Out popped two soldiers with great battleaxes in their hands and looking as fierce as dragons. 'Are you a stranger in this town?' said one in a great, gruff voice.

'Yes,' said the beggar, 'I am.'

'And where are you going?'

'I am going into the town.'

'No, you are not.'

'Why not?'

'Because no stranger enters here. Yonder is the pathway. You must take that if you would enter the town.'

'Very well,' said the beggar, 'I would just as lief go into the town that way as another.'

So off he marched without another word. On and on he went along the narrow pathway until at last he came to a little gate of polished brass. Over the gate were written these words, in great letters as red as blood:

'Who Enters here Shall Surely Die.'

Many and many a man besides the beggar had travelled that path and looked up at those letters, and when he had read them had turned and gone away again. But the beggar neither turned nor went away; because why, he could neither read nor write a word, and so the blood-red letters had no fear for him. Up he marched to the brazen gate, as boldly as though it had been a kitchen door, and rap! tap! tap! he knocked upon it. He waited awhile, but nobody came. Rap! tap! tap! he knocked again; and then, after a little while, for the third time—Rap! tap! tap! Then instantly the gate swung open and he entered. So soon as he had crossed the threshold it was banged to behind him again, just as the garden gate had been when the king had first sent for him. He found himself in a long, dark entry, and at the end of it another door, and over it the same words, written in blood-red letters:

'Beware! Beware! Who Enters here Shall Surely Die!'

'Well,' said the beggar, 'this is the hardest town for a body to come into that I ever saw.' And then he opened the second door and passed through.

It was fit to deafen a body! Such a shout the beggar's ears had never heard before; such a sight the beggar's eyes had never beheld, for there, before him, was a great splendid hall of marble as white as snow. All along the hall stood scores of lords and ladies in silks and satins, and with jewels on their necks and arms fit to dazzle a body's eyes. Right up the middle of the hall stretched a carpet of blue velvet, and at the farther end, on a throne of gold, sat a lady as beautiful as the sun and moon and all the stars.

'Welcome! Welcome!' they all shouted, until the beggar was nearly deafened by the noise they all made, and the lady herself stood up and smiled upon him.

Then there came three young men, and led the beggar up the carpet of velvet to the throne of gold.

'Welcome, my hero!' said the beautiful lady; 'and have you, then, come at last?'

'Yes,' said the beggar, 'I have.'

'Long have I waited for you,' said the lady; 'long have I waited for the hero who would dare without fear to come through the two gates of death to marry me and to rule as king over this country, and now at last you are here.'

'Yes,' said the beggar, 'I am.'

Meanwhile, while all these things were happening, the king of that other country had painted out the words his father had written on the walls, and had had these words painted in in their stead:

'All Things are as Man does.'

For a while he was very well satisfied with them, until, a week after, he was bidden to the wedding of the Queen of the

Golden Mountains; for when he came there who should the bridegroom be but the beggar whom he had set adrift in the wooden box a week or so before.

The bridegroom winked at him, but said never a word, good or ill, for he was willing to let all that had happened be past and gone. But the king saw how matters stood as clear as daylight, and when he got back home again he had the new words that stood on the walls of the room painted out, and had the old ones painted in in bigger letters than ever:

'All Things are as Fate wills.'

2

CLAUS AND HIS WONDERFUL STAFF

Hans and Claus were born brothers. Hans was the elder and Claus was the younger; Hans was the richer and Claus was the poorer—that is the way that the world goes sometimes.

Everything was easy for Hans at home; he drank much beer, and had sausages and white bread three times a day; but Claus worked and worked, and no luck came of it—that, also, is the way that the world goes sometimes.

One time Claus spoke to Hans of this matter. 'See, Hans,' said he, 'you should give me some money, for that which belongs to one brother should help the other.'

But Hans saw through different colored spectacles than Claus. No; he would do nothing of the kind. If Claus wanted money he had better go out into, the world to look for it; for some folks said that money was rolling about in the wide world like peas on a threshing floor. So said Hans, for Claus was so poor that Hans was ashamed of him, and wanted him to leave home so as to be rid of him for good and all.

This was how Claus came to go out into the world.

But before he went, he cut himself a good stout staff of hazel wood to help his heavy feet over the road.

Now the staff that Claus had cut was a rod of witch hazel, which has the power of showing wherever treasure lies buried.

But Claus knew no more of that than the chick in the shell.

So off he went into the world, walking along with great contentment, kicking up little clouds of dust at every step, and whistling as gayly as though trouble had never been hatched from mares' eggs. By and by, he came to the great town, and then he went to the marketplace and stood, with many others, with a straw in his mouth—for that meant that he wanted to take service with somebody.

Presently there came along an old, old man, bent almost double with the weight of the years which he carried upon his shoulders. This was a famous doctor of the black arts. He had read as many as a hundred books, so that he was more learned than any man in all of the world—even the minister of the village. He knew, as well as the birds know when the cherries are ripe, that Claus had a stick of witch hazel, so he came to the marketplace, peering here and peering there, just as honest folks do when they are looking for a servant. After a while he came to where Claus was, and then he stopped in front of him. 'Do you want to take service, my friend?' said he.

Yes, that was what Claus wanted; why else should he stand in the marketplace with a straw in his mouth?

Well, they bargained and bargained, and talked and talked, and the end of the matter was that Claus agreed to sell his services to the old master of black arts for seven pennies a week. So they made their bargain, and off went the master with Claus at his heels. After they had come a little distance away from the crowd at the marketplace, the master of black arts asked Claus where he had got that fine staff of hazel.

'Oh, I got it over yonder,' said Claus, pointing with his thumb.

But could he find the place again?

Well, Claus did not know how about that; perhaps he could, and perhaps he could not.

But suppose that Claus had a thaler in his hand, *then* could he find the place again?

Oh yes; in that case Claus was almost sure that he could find the place again.

So good. Then here was a bottle of yellow water. If Claus would take the bottle of yellow water, and pour it over the stump from which he had cut his staff, there would come seven green snakes out of a hole at the foot of the hazel bush. After these seven snakes, there would come a white snake, with a golden crown on its head, from out of the same hole. Now if Claus would catch that white snake in the empty bottle, and bring it to the master of black-arts, he should have not one thaler, but two—that was what the master said.

Oh yes, Claus could do that; that was no such hard thing. So he took the bottle of yellow water and off he went.

By and by he came to the place where he had cut his hazel twig. There he did as the master of black arts had told him; he poured the yellow water over the stump of hazel from which he had cut his staff. Then everything happened just as the other had said: first there came seven green snakes out of the hole at the foot of the hazel bush, and after they had all gone, there came a white snake, with a little golden crown on its head, and with its body gleaming like real silver. Then Claus caught the white snake, and put it into the bottle and corked it up tightly. After he had done this he went back to the master of black arts again.

Now this white snake was what the folk call a tomtsnake in that land. Whoever eats of a broth made of it can understand the language of all the birds of the air and all the beasts of the field; so nobody need wonder that the master was as glad as glad could be to have his white snake safe and sound.

He bade Claus build a fire of dry wood, and as soon as there was a good blaze he set a pot of water upon it to boil. When the water in the pot began to boil, he chopped up the white snake into little pieces and threw them into it. So the snake boiled and boiled and boiled, and Claus stared with wonder as though he would never shut his eyes again.

Now it happened that just about the time that the broth was cooked, the master was called out of the room for this or for that. No sooner was his back turned than Claus began to wonder what the broth was like. 'I will just have a little taste,' said he to himself; 'surely it can do no harm to the rest of the soup.' So he stuck his finger first into the broth and then into his mouth; but what the broth tasted like he never could tell, for just then the master came in again, and Claus was so frightened at what he had done that he had no wits to think of the taste of anything.

Presently the master of black arts went to the pot of broth, and, taking off the lid, began smelling of it. But no sooner had he sniffed a smell of the steam than he began thumping his head with his knuckles, and tearing his hair, and stamping his feet. 'Somebody's had a finger in my broth!!!' he roared. For the master knew at once that all the magic had been taken out of it by the touch of Claus's finger.

As for poor Claus, he was so frightened that he fell upon his knees, and began begging: 'Oh! Dear master—' But he got no further than this, for the master bawled at him,

'You have taken the best,

You may have the rest.'

And so saying, he threw pot and broth and all at Claus, so that if he hadn't ducked his head he might have been scalded to death. Then Claus ran out into the street, for he saw that there was no place for him to stay in that house.

Now in the street there was a cock and a hen, scratching and clucking together in the dust, and Claus understood every word that they said to each other, so he stopped and listened to them.

This is what they said:

The cock said to the hen, 'Yonder goes our new serving man.'

And the hen said to the cock, 'Yes, yonder he goes.'

And the cock said to the hen, 'He is leaving the best behind him.'

And the hen said to the cock, 'What is it that he is leaving?'

And the cock said to the hen, 'He is leaving behind him the witch hazel staff that he brought with him.'

And the hen said to the cock, 'Yes, that is so. He would be a fool to leave that behind, yet he is not the first one to think that peas are pebbles.'

As for Claus, you can guess how he opened his eyes, for he saw how the land lay, and that he had other ears than he had before.

'Hui!' said he, 'that is good! I have bought more for my penny than I had in my bargain.'

As for the hazel staff, he was not going to leave that behind, you may be sure. So he sneaked about the place till he laid hand on it again; then he stepped away, right foot foremost, for he did not know what the master of black arts might do to him if he should catch him.

Well, after he had left the town, he went along, tramp! tramp! tramp! until, by and by, he grew tired and sat down beneath an oak tree to rest himself.

Now, as he sat there, looking up through the leaves, thinking of nothing at all, two ravens came flying and lit in the tree above him. After a while the ravens began talking together, and this was what they said:

The one raven said, 'Yonder is poor Claus sitting below us.'

And the other raven said, '*Poor* Claus, did you say, brother? Do you not see the witch hazel lying on the ground beside him?'

The one raven said, 'Oh yes; I see that, but what good does it do him?'

And the other raven said, 'It does him no good now, but if he were to go home again and strike on the great stone on the top of the hill back of Herr Axel's house, then it would do him good; for in it lies a great treasure of silver and gold.'

Claus had picked up his ears at all this talk, you may be sure. 'See,' said he, 'that is the way that a man will pass by a great fortune in the little world at home to seek for a little fortune in the great world abroad'—which was all very true. After that he lost no time in getting back home again.

'What! Are you back again?' said Hans.

'Oh yes,' said Claus, 'I am back again.'

'That is always the way with a pewter penny,' said Hans—for that is how some of us are welcomed home after we have been away.

As for Claus, he was as full of thoughts as an egg is of meat, but he said nothing of them to Hans. Off he went to the high hill back of Herr Axel's house, and there, sure enough, was the great stone at the very top of the hill.

Claus struck on the stone with his oaken staff, and it opened like the door of a beer vault, for all was blackness within. A flight of steps led down below, and down the steps Claus went. But when he had come to the bottom of the steps, he stared till his eyes were like great round saucers; for there stood sacks of gold and silver, piled up like bags of grain in the malthouse.

At one end of the room was a great stone seat, and on the seat sat a little manikin smoking a pipe. As for the beard of the little man, it was as long as he was short, for it hung down so far that part of it touched the stone floor.

'How do you find yourself, Claus?' said the little manikin, calling Claus by his name.

'So good!' said Claus, taking off his hat to the other.

'And what would you like to have, Claus?' said the little man.

'I would like,' said Claus, 'to have some money, if you please.'

'Take what you want,' said the little man, 'only do not forget to take the best with you.'

Oh no; Claus would not forget the best; so he held the staff tighter than ever in his fist—for what could be better than the staff that brought him there? So he went here and there, filling his pockets with the gold and silver money till they bulged out like the pockets of a thief in the orchard; but all the time he kept tight hold of his staff, I can tell you.

When he had as much as his pockets could hold, he thanked the little manikin and went his way, and the stone door closed behind him.

And now Claus lived like a calf in the green cornfield. Everything he had was of the best, and he had twice as much of that as any of the neighbors. Then how brother Hans stared and scratched his head and wondered, when he saw how Claus sat in the sun all day, doing nothing but smoking his pipe and eating of the best, as though he were a born prince! Every day Claus went to the little man in the hill with his pockets empty, and came back with them stuffed with gold and silver money. At last he had so much that he could not count it, and so he had to send over to brother Hans for his quart pot, so that he might measure it.

But Hans was cunning. 'I will see what makes brother Claus so well-off in the world all of a sudden,' said he; so he smeared the inside of the quart pot with bird lime.

Then Claus measured his gold and silver money in Hans's quart pot, and when he was done with it he sent it back again. But more went back with the quart pot than came with it, for two gold pieces stuck to the birdlime, and it was these that went back with the pot to brother Hans.

'What!' cried Hans, 'has that stupid Claus found so much money that he has to measure it in a quart pot? We must see the inside of this business!' So off he went to Claus's house, and there he found Claus sitting in the sun and smoking his pipe, just as though he owned all of the world.

'Where did you get all that money, Claus?' said Hans.

Oh! Claus could not tell him that.

But Hans was bound to know all about it, so he begged and begged so prettily that at last Claus had to tell him everything. Then, of course, nothing would do but Hans must have a try with the hazel staff also.

Well, Claus made no words at that. He was a good natured fellow, and surely there was enough for both. So the upshot of the matter was that Hans marched off with the hazel staff.

But Hans was no such simpleton as Claus; no, not he. Oh no, he would not take all that trouble for two poor pocketfuls of money. He would have a bagful; no, he would have two bagfuls. So he slung two meal sacks over his shoulder, and off he started for the hill back of Herr Axel's house.

When he came to the stone he knocked upon it, and it opened to him just as it had done for Claus. Down he went into the pit, and there sat the little old manikin, just as he had done from the very first.

'How do you find yourself, Hans?' said the little old manikin.

Oh, Hans found himself very well. Might he have some of the money that stood around the room in the sacks?

Yes, that he might; only remember to take the best away with him.

Prut! Teach a dog to eat sausages. Hans would see that he took the best, trust him for that. So he filled the bags full of gold, and never touched the silver—for, surely, gold is better than anything else in the world, says Hans to himself. So, when he had filled his two bags with gold, and had shaken the pieces well down, he flung the one over one shoulder, and the other over the other, and then he had as much as he could carry. As for the staff of witch hazel, he let it lie where it was, for he only had two hands and they were both full.

But Hans never got his two bags of gold away from the vault, for just as he was leaving—bang! came the stone together, and caught him as though he was a mouse in the door; and that was an end of him. That happened because he left the witch hazel behind.

That was the way in which Claus came to lose his magic staff; but that did not matter much, for he had enough to live on and to spare. So he married the daughter of the Herr Baron (for he might marry whom he chose, now that he was rich), and after that he lived as happy as a fly on the warm chimney.

Now, this is so—it is better to take a little away at a time and carry your staff with you, than to take all at once and leave it behind.

3

CLEVER PETER AND THE TWO BOTTLES

'Yes, Peter is clever.' So said his mother; but then every goose thinks her own gosling a swan.

The minister and all of the people of the village said Peter was but a dull block. Maybe Peter was a fool; but, as the old saying goes, never a fool tumbles out of the tree but he lights on his toes. So now you shall hear how that Peter sold his two baskets of eggs for more than you or I could do, wise as we be.

'Peter,' said his mother.

'Yes,' said Peter, for he was well brought up, and always answered when he was spoken to.

'My dear little child, thou art wise, though so young now; how shall we get money to pay our rent?'

'Sell the eggs that the speckled hen has laid,' said Peter.

'But when we have spent the money for them, what then?'

'Sell more eggs,' said Peter, for he had an answer for everything.

'But when the speckled hen lays no more eggs, what shall we do then?'

'We shall see,' said Peter.

'Now indeed art thou wise,' said his mother, 'and I take

thy meaning; it is this, when we have spent all, we must do as the little birds do, and trust in the good heaven.' Peter meant nothing of the kind, but then folks will think that such wise fellows as Peter and I mean more than we say, whence comes our wisdom.

So the next day Peter started off to the town, with the basket full of nice white eggs. The day was bright and warm and fair; the wind blew softly, and the wheat fields lay like green velvet in the sun. The flowers were sprinkled all over the grass, and the bees kicked up their yellow legs as they tilted into them. The garlic stuck up stout spikes into the air, and the young radishes were green and lusty. The brown bird in the tree sang, 'Cuckoo! Cuckoo!' and Peter trudged contentedly along, kicking up little clouds of dust at every footstep, whistling merrily and staring up into the bright sky, where the white clouds hung like little sheep, feeding on the wide blue field. 'If those clouds were sheep, and the sheep were mine, then I would be a great man and very proud,' said Peter. But the clouds were clouds, and he was not a great man; nevertheless, he whistled more merrily than ever, for it was very nice to think of these things.

So he trudged along with great comfort until high noontide, against which time he had come nigh to the town, for he could see the red roofs and the tall spires peeping over the crest of the next green hill. By this time his stomach was crying, 'Give! Give!' for it longed for bread and cheese. Now, a great grey stone stood near by at the forking of the road, and just as Peter came to it he heard a noise. 'Click! Clack!' he turned his head, and, lo and behold! the side of the stone opened like a door, and out came a little old man dressed all in fine black velvet. 'Good day, Peter,' said he. 'Good day, sir,' said Peter, and he took off his hat as he spoke, for he could see with half an eye that this little old gentleman was none of your cheese-paring fine folks.

'Will you strike a bargain with me for your eggs?' said the

little old man. Yes, Peter would strike a bargain; what would the little gentleman give him for his eggs? 'I will give you this,' said the little old man, and he drew a black bottle out of his pocket.

Peter took the bottle and turned it over and over in his hands. 'It is,' said he, 'a pretty little, good little, sweet little bottle, but it is not worth as much as my basket of eggs.'

'Prut!' said the little gentleman, 'now you are not talking like the wise Peter. You should never judge by the outside of things. What would you like to have?'

'I should like,' said Peter, 'to have a good dinner.'

'Nothing easier!' said the little gentleman, and he drew the cork. Pop! pop! and what should come out of the bottle but two tall men, dressed all in blue with gold trimmings. 'What will you have, sir?' said the first of these to the little gentleman.

'A good dinner for two,' said the little man.

No sooner said than done; for, before you could say Frederic Strutzenwillenbachen, there stood a table, with a sweet, clean, white cloth spread over it, and on this was the nicest dinner that you ever saw, for there were beer and chitterlings, and cheese and good white bread, fit for the king. Then Peter and the little man fell to with might and main, and ate till they could eat no more. After they were done, the two tall men took table and dishes and all back into the bottle again, and the little gentleman corked it up.

'Yes,' said Peter, 'I will give you my basket of eggs for the little black bottle.' And so the bargain was struck. Then Peter started off home, and the little man went back again into the great stone and closed the door behind him. He took the basket of eggs with him; where he took it neither Peter nor I will ever be able to tell you.

So Peter trudged along homeward, until, after a while, the day waxing warm, he grew tired. 'I wish,' said he, 'that I had a fine white horse to ride.'

Then he took the cork out of the bottle. Pop! pop! and out came the two tall fellows, just as they had done for the little old man. 'What will you have, sir?' said the first of them.

'I will have,' said Peter, 'a fine white horse to ride.'

No sooner said than done; for there, before him in the road, stood a fine white horse, with a long mane and tail, just like so much spun silk. In his mouth was a silver bit; on his back was a splendid saddle, covered all over with gold and jewels; on his feet were shoes of pure gold, so that he was a very handsome horse indeed.

Peter mounted on his great horse and rode away home, as grand as though he were a lord or a nobleman.

Every one whom he met stopped in the middle of the road and looked after him. 'Just look at Peter!' cried they; but Peter held his chin very high, and rode along without looking at them, for he knew what a fine sight he was on his white horse.

And so he came home again.

'What didst thou get for thy eggs, my little duck?' said his mother.

'I got a bottle, mother,' said Peter.

Then at first Peter's mother began to think as others thought, that Peter was a dull block. But when she saw what a wonderful bottle it was, and how it held many good things and one over, she changed her mind again, and thought that her Peter was as wise as the moon.

And now nothing was lacking in the cottage; if Peter and his mother wanted this, it came to them; if they wished for that, the two tall men in the bottle fetched it. They lined the house all inside with pure gold, and built the chimneys of bricks of silver, so that there was nothing so fine between all the four great rivers. Peter dressed in satin and his mother in silk, and everybody called him 'Lord Peter'. Even the minister of the village said that he was no dull boy, for nobody is dull who rides on horseback and never wears wooden shoes. So now Peter was a rich man.

One morning Peter said to his mother, 'Mother, I am going to ask the king to let me marry his daughter.'

To this his mother said nothing, for surely her Peter was as good as any princess that ever lived.

So off Peter rode, dressed all in his best and seated astride of a grand horse. At last he came to the palace which was finer than the handsome new house of Herr Mayor Kopff. Rap! rap! rap! Peter knocked at the door, and presently came a neat servant girl and opened it to him. 'Is the king at home, my dear?' said Peter.

Yes, the king was at home; would he come into the parlour and sit down? So Peter went into the parlour and sat down, and then the king came in, dressed all in his best dressing gown, with silver slippers upon his feet, and a golden crown upon his head.

'What is your name?' said the king.

'Peter Stultzenmilchen,' said Peter.

'And what do you want, Lord Peter,' said the king; for, as I have said, Peter was dressed in his best clothes, and the old king thought that he was a great lord.

'I want to marry your daughter,' said Peter.

To this the king said 'Hum-m-m,' and Peter said nothing. Then the king said that he had determined that no one should marry his daughter without bringing him a basketful of diamonds, rubies, topazes, emeralds, pearls, and all manner of precious stones; for he thought by this to get rid of Peter.

'Is that all?' said Peter. 'Nothing is easier.'

So off he went, until he came to a chestnut woods just back of the royal kitchen garden. There he uncorked his bottle. Pop! pop! and out came the two tall men. 'What will you have, sir?' said they. Peter told them what he wanted, and it was no sooner said than done; for, there on the ground before him, stood a basketful of all kinds of precious stones; each of them was as large as a hen's egg, and over all of them was spread a nice clean white napkin. So Peter took the basket on his arm and went back again to the palace.

But how the king did open his eyes, to be sure, and how he stared! 'Now,' said Peter, 'I should like to marry your daughter, if you please.'

At this the king hemmed and hawed again. No, Peter could not marry the princess yet, for the king had determined that no man should marry his daughter without bringing him a bird all of pure silver that could sing whenever it was wanted, and that more sweetly than a nightingale; for he thought that now he should be rid of Peter, at any rate.

'Nothing easier,' said Peter, and off he went again.

When he had come to the chestnut woods, he uncorked his bottle and told the two tall men what he wanted. No sooner said than done; for there was a bird all of pure silver. And not only that, but the bird sat in a little golden tree, and the leaves of the tree were emeralds, and rubies hung like cherries from the branches.

Then Peter wrapped this up in his handkerchief and took it to the palace. As for the king, he could not look at it or listen to it enough.

'Now,' said Peter, 'I should like to marry your daughter, if you please.'

But at this the king sang the same tune again. No, Peter could not marry his daughter yet, for the king had determined that the man who was to marry his daughter should first bring him a golden sword, so keen that it could cut a feather floating in the air, yet so strong that it could cut through an iron bar.

'Nothing easier,' said Peter, and this time the men of the bottle brought him such a sword as he asked for, and the hilt was studded all over with precious stones, so that it was very handsome indeed. Then Peter brought it to the king, and it did as the king would have it—it cut through a feather floating in the air; as for the iron bar, it cut through that as easily as you would bite through a radish.

And now it seemed as though there was nothing else to be done but to let Peter marry the princess. So the king asked him in to supper, and they all three sat down together, the king and the princess and Peter. And it was a fine feast, I can tell you, for they had both white and red wine, besides sausages and cheese, and real white bread and puddings, and all manner of good things; for kings and princesses eat and drink of the best.

As for Peter, he made eyes at the princess, and the princess looked down on her plate and blushed, and Peter thought that he had never seen such a pretty girl.

After a while the king began to question Peter how he came by all these fine things—the precious stones, the silver bird, and the golden sword; but no, Peter would not tell. Then the king and the princess begged and begged him, until, at last, Peter lost his wits and told all about the bottle. Then the king said nothing more, and presently, it being nine o'clock, Peter went to bed. After he had gone the king and the princess put their heads together, and the end of the matter was that the wicked king went to Peter's room and stole the bottle from under the pillow where he had hidden it, and put one in its place that was as empty as a beer barrel after the soldiers have been in the town; for the king and the princess thought that it would be a fine thing to have the bottle for themselves.

When the next morning had come, and they were all sitting at their breakfast together, the king said, 'Now, Lord Peter, let us see what your bottle will do; give us such and such a kind of wine.'

'Nothing easier,' said Peter. Then he uncorked the bottle,

but not so much as a single dead fly came out of it.

'But where is the wine?' said the king.

'I do not know,' said Peter.

At this the king called him hard names and turned him out of the palace, neck and heels; so back poor Peter went to his mother with a flea in his ear, as the saying is. Now he was poor again, and everybody called him a dull block, for he rode no great white horse and he wore wooden shoes.

'Never mind,' said his mother, 'here is another basket of eggs from the speckled hen.' So Peter set off with these to the market town, as he had done with the others before. When he had come to the great stone at the forking of the road, whom should he meet but the same little gentleman he had met the first time. 'Will you strike a bargain?' said he. Yes, Peter would strike a bargain, and gladly. Thereupon the little old man brought out another black bottle.

'Two men are in this bottle,' said the little old man; 'when they have done all that you want them to do, say 'brikket-ligg' and they will go back again. Will you trade with me?' Yes, Peter would trade. So Peter gave the little man the eggs, and the little man gave Peter the second bottle, and they parted very good friends.

After a while Peter grew tired. 'Now,' said he to himself, 'I will ride a little'; and so he drew the cork out of the bottle. Pop! pop! out came two men from the bottle; but this time they were ugly and black, and each held a stout stick in his hand. They said not a word, but, without more ado, fell upon Peter and began threshing him as though he was wheat on the barn floor. 'Stop! Stop!' cried Peter, and he went hopping and skipping up and down, and here and there, but it seemed as though the two ugly black men did not hear him, for the blows fell as thick as hail on the roof. At last he gathered his wits together, like a flock of pigeons, and cried, 'Brikket-ligg! Brikket-ligg!' Then, whisk! pop!

they went back into the bottle again, and Peter corked it up, and corked it tightly, I can tell you.

The next day he started off to the palace once more. Rap! rap! rap! he knocked at the door. Was the king at home? Yes, the king was at home; would he come and sit in the parlour?

Presently the king came in, in dressing gown and slippers. 'What! Are you back again?' said he.

'Yes; I am back again,' said Peter.

'What do you want?' said the king.

'I want to marry the princess,' said Peter.

'What have you brought this time?' said the king.

'I have brought another bottle,' said Peter.

Then the king rubbed his hands and was very polite indeed, and asked Peter in to breakfast, and Peter went. So they all three sat down together, the king, the princess, and Peter.

'My dear,' said the king, to the princess, 'the Lord Peter has brought another bottle with him.' Thereat the princess was very polite also. Would Lord Peter let them see the bottle? Oh yes! Peter would do that: so he drew it out of his pocket and sat it upon the table.

Perhaps they would like to have it opened. Yes, that they would. So Peter opened the bottle.

Hui! What a hubbub there was! The king hopped about till his slippers flew off, his dressing gown fluttered like great wings, and his crown rolled off from his head and across the floor, like a quoit at the fair. As for the princess, she never danced in all of her life as she danced that morning. They made such a noise that the soldiers of the Royal Guard came running in; but the two tall black men spared them no more than the king and the princess. Then came all of the Lords of the Council, and they likewise danced to the same music as the rest.

'Oh, Peter! Dear Lord Peter! Cork up your men again!' they all cried.

'Will you give me back my bottle?' said Peter.
'Yes! yes!' cried the king.
'Will you marry me?' said Peter.
'Yes! yes!' cried the princess.

Then Peter said 'brikket-ligg!' and the two tall men popped back into the bottle again. So the king gave him back his other bottle, and the minister was called in and married him to the princess.

After that he lived happily, and when the old king died he became king over all of the land. As for the princess, she was as good a wife as you ever saw, but Peter always kept the bottle near to him—maybe that was the reason.

Ah me! If I could only take my eggs to such a
market and get two such bottles for them!
What would I do with them? It would
take too long to tell you.

4

THE ENCHANTED ISLAND

But it is not always the lucky one that carries away the plums; sometimes he only shakes the tree, and the wise man pockets the fruit.

Once upon a long, long time ago, and in a country far, far away, there lived two men in the same town and both were named Selim; one was Selim the Baker and one was Selim the Fisherman.

Selim the Baker was well off in the world, but Selim the Fisherman was only so-so. Selim the Baker always had plenty to eat and a warm corner in cold weather, but many and many a time Selim the Fisherman's stomach went empty and his teeth went chattering.

Once it happened that for time after time Selim the Fisherman caught nothing but bad luck in his nets, and not so much as a single sprat, and he was very hungry. 'Come,' said he to himself, 'those who have some should surely give to those who have none,' and so he went to Selim the Baker. 'Let me have a loaf of bread,' said he, 'and I will pay you for it tomorrow.'

'Very well,' said Selim the Baker; 'I will let you have a loaf of bread, if you will give me all that you catch in your nets tomorrow.'

'So be it,' said Selim the Fisherman, for need drives one to hard bargains sometimes; and therewith he got his loaf of bread.

So the next day Selim the Fisherman fished and fished and fished and fished, and still he caught no more than the day before; until just at sunset he cast his net for the last time for the day, and, lo and behold! There was something heavy in it. So he dragged it ashore, and what should it be but a leaden box, sealed as tight as wax, and covered with all manner of strange letters and figures. 'Here,' said he, 'is something to pay for my bread of yesterday, at any rate;' and as he was an honest man, off he marched with it to Selim the Baker.

They opened the box in the baker's shop, and within they found two rolls of yellow linen. In each of the rolls of linen was another little leaden box: in one was a finger ring of gold set with a red stone, in the other was a finger ring of iron set with nothing at all.

That was all the box held; nevertheless, that was the greatest catch that ever any fisherman made in the world; for, though Selim the one or Selim the other knew no more of the matter than the cat under the stove, the gold ring was the Ring of Luck and the iron ring was the Ring of Wisdom.

Inside of the gold ring were carved these letters: 'Whosoever wears me, shall have that which all men seek—for so it is with good luck in this world.'

Inside of the iron ring were written these words: 'Whosoever wears me, shall have that which few men care for—and that is the way it is with wisdom in our town.'

'Well,' said Selim the Baker, and he slipped the gold ring of good luck on his finger, 'I have driven a good bargain, and you have paid for your loaf of bread.'

'But what will you do with the other ring?' said Selim the Fisherman.

'Oh, you may have that,' said Selim the Baker.

Well, that evening, as Selim the Baker sat in front of his shop in the twilight smoking a pipe of tobacco, the ring he wore began to work. Up came a little old man with a white beard, and he was dressed all in grey from top to toe, and he wore a black velvet cap, and he carried a long staff in his hand. He stopped in front of Selim the Baker, and stood looking at him a long, long time. At last—'Is your name Selim?' said he.

'Yes,' said Selim the Baker, 'it is.'

'And do you wear a gold ring with a red stone on your finger?'

'Yes,' said Selim, 'I do.'

'Then come with me,' said the little old man, 'and I will show you the wonder of the world.'

'Well,' said Selim the Baker, 'that will be worth the seeing, at any rate.' So he emptied out his pipe of tobacco, and put on his hat and followed the way the old man led.

Up one street they went, and down another, and here and there through alleys and byways where Selim had never been before. At last they came to where a high wall ran along the narrow street, with a garden behind it, and by and by to an iron gate. The old man rapped upon the gate three times with his knuckles, and cried in a loud voice, 'Open to Selim, who wears the Ring of Luck!'

Then instantly the gate swung open, and Selim the Baker followed the old man into the garden.

Bang! shut the gate behind him, and there he was.

There he was! And such a place he had never seen before. Such fruit! Such flowers! Such fountains! Such summer houses!

'This is nothing,' said the old man; 'this is only the beginning of wonder. Come with me.'

He led the way down a long pathway between the trees, and Selim followed. By and by, far away, they saw the light of torches; and when they came to what they saw, lo and behold! There was the sea shore, and a boat with four-and-twenty oarsmen, each dressed in cloth of gold and silver more splendidly than a prince. And there were four-and-twenty black slaves, carrying each a torch of spice wood, so that all the air was filled with sweet smells. The old man led the way, and Selim, following, entered the boat; and there was a seat for him made soft with satin cushions embroidered with gold and precious stones and stuffed with down, and Selim wondered whether he was not dreaming.

The oarsmen pushed off from the shore and away they rowed.

On they rowed and on they rowed for all that livelong night.

At last morning broke, and then as the sun rose Selim saw such a sight as never mortal eyes beheld before or since. It was the wonder of wonders—a great city built on an island. The island was all one mountain; and on it, one above another and another above that again, stood palaces that glistened like snow, and orchards of fruit, and gardens of flowers and green trees.

And as the boat came nearer and nearer to the city, Selim could see that all around on the house tops and down to the water's edge were crowds and crowds of people. All were looking out towards the sea, and when they saw the boat and Selim in it, a great shout went up like the roaring of rushing waters.

'It is the king!' they cried—'it is the king! It is Selim the king!'

Then the boat landed, and there stood dozens of scores of great princes and nobles to welcome Selim when he came ashore. And there was a white horse waiting for him to ride, and its saddle and bridle were studded with diamonds and rubies and emeralds that sparkled and glistened like the stars in heaven, and Selim thought for sure he must be dreaming with his eyes open.

But he was not dreaming, for it was all as true as that eggs are eggs. So up the hill he rode, and to the grandest and the most splendid of all the splendid palaces, the princes and noblemen riding with him, and the crowd shouting as though to split their throats.

And what a palace it was!—as white as snow and painted all inside with gold and blue. All around it were gardens blooming with fruit and flowers, and the like of it mortal man never saw in the world before.

There they made a king of Selim, and put a golden crown on his head; and that is what the Ring of Good Luck can do for a baker.

But wait a bit! There was something queer about it all, and that is now to be told.

All that day was feasting and drinking and merrymaking, and the twinging and twanging of music, and dancing of beautiful dancing girls, and such things as Selim had never heard tell of in all his life before. And when night came they lit thousands and thousands of candles of perfumed wax; so that it was a hard matter to say when night began and day ended, only that the one smelled sweeter than the other.

But at last it came midnight, and then suddenly, in an instant, all the lights went out and everything was as dark as pitch—not a spark, not a glimmer anywhere. And, just as suddenly, all the sound of music and dancing and merrymaking ceased, and everybody began to wail and cry until it was enough to wring one's heart to hear. Then, in the midst of all the wailing and crying, a door was flung open, and in came six tall and terrible black men, dressed all in black from top to toe, carrying each a flaming torch; and by the light of the torches King Selim saw that all—the princes, the noblemen, the dancing girls—all lay on their faces on the floor.

The six men took King Selim—who shuddered and shook

with fear—by the arms, and marched him through dark, gloomy entries and passageways, until they came at last to the very heart of the palace.

There was a great high vaulted room all of black marble, and in the middle of it was a pedestal with seven steps, all of black marble; and on the pedestal stood a stone statue of a woman looking as natural as life, only that her eyes were shut. The statue was dressed like a queen: she wore a golden crown on her head, and upon her body hung golden robes, set with diamonds and emeralds and rubies and sapphires and pearls and all sorts of precious stones.

As for the face of the statue, white paper and black ink could not tell you how beautiful it was. When Selim looked at it, it made his heart stand still in his breast, it was so beautiful.

The six men brought Selim up in front of the statue, and then a voice came as though from the vaulted roof: 'Selim! Selim! Selim!' it said, 'what are thou doing? Today is feasting and drinking and merrymaking, but beware of tomorrow!'

As soon as these words were ended the six black men marched King Selim back whence they had brought him; there they left him and passed out one by one as they had first come in, and the door shut to behind them.

Then in an instant the lights flashed out again, the music began to play and the people began to talk and laugh, and King Selim thought that maybe all that had just passed was only a bit of an ugly dream after all.

So that is the way King Selim the Baker began to reign, and that is the way he continued to reign. All day was feasting and drinking and making merry and music and laughing and talking. But every night at midnight the same thing happened: the lights went out, all the people began wailing and crying, and the six tall, terrible black men came with flashing torches and marched King Selim away to the beautiful statue. And every night the same voice said—'Selim! Selim! Selim! What art thou doing! Today is feasting and drinking and merrymaking; but beware of tomorrow!'

So things went on for a twelvemonth, and at last came the end of the year. That day and night the merrymaking was merrier and wilder and madder than it had ever been before, but the great clock in the tower went on—tick, tock! tick, tock!—and by and by it came midnight. Then, as it always happened before, the lights went out, and all was as black as ink. But this time there was no wailing and crying out, but everything was silent as death; the door opened slowly, and in came, not six black men as before, but nine men as silent as death, dressed all in flaming red, and the torches they carried burned as red as blood. They took King Selim by the arms, just as the six men had done, and marched him through the same entries and passageways, and so came at last to the same vaulted room. There stood the statue, but now it was turned to flesh and blood, and the eyes were open and looking straight at Selim the Baker.

'Art thou Selim?' said she; and she pointed her finger straight at him.

'Yes, I am Selim,' said he.

'And dost thou wear the gold ring with the red stone?' said she.

'Yes,' said he; 'I have it on my finger.'

'And dost thou wear the iron ring?'

'No,' said he; 'I gave that to Selim the Fisherman.'

The words had hardly left his lips when the statue gave a great cry and clapped her hands together. In an instant an echoing cry sounded all over the town—a shriek fit to split the ears.

The next moment there came another sound—a sound like thunder—above and below and everywhere. The earth began to shake and to rock, and the houses began to topple and fall, and the people began to scream and to yell and to shout, and the waters of the sea began to lash and to roar, and the wind began to bellow and howl. Then it was a good thing for King Selim that he wore Luck's Ring; for, though all the beautiful snow-white palace about him and above him began to crumble to pieces like slaked lime, the sticks and the stones and the beams to fall this side of him and that, he crawled out from under it without a scratch or a bruise, like a rat out of a cellar.

That is what Luck's Ring did for him.

But his troubles were not over yet; for, just as he came out from under all the ruin, the island began to sink down into the water, carrying everything along with it—that is, everything but him and one thing else. That one other thing was an empty boat, and King Selim climbed into it, and nothing else saved him from drowning. It was Luck's Ring that did that for him also.

The boat floated on and on until it came to another island that was just like the island he had left, only that there was neither tree nor blade of grass nor hide nor hair nor living thing of any kind. Nevertheless, it was an island just like the other: a high mountain and nothing else. There Selim the Baker went ashore, and there he would have starved to death only for Luck's Ring; for one day a boat came sailing by, and when poor Selim shouted, those aboard heard him and came and took him off. How they all stared to see his golden crown—for he still wore it—and his robes of silk and satin and the gold and jewels!

Before they would consent to carry him away, they made him give up all the fine things he had. Then they took him home again to the town whence he had first come, just as poor as when he had started. Back he went to his bake shop and his ovens, and the first thing he did was to take off his gold ring and put it on the shelf.

'If that is the ring of good luck,' said he, 'I do not want to wear the like of it.'

That is the way with mortal man: for one has to have the Ring of Wisdom as well, to turn the Ring of Luck to good account.

And now for Selim the Fisherman.

Well, thus it happened to him. For a while he carried the iron ring around in his pocket—just as so many of us do—without thinking to put it on. But one day he slipped it on his finger—and that is what we do not all of us do. After that he never took it off again, and the world went smoothly with him. He was not rich, but then he was not poor; he was not merry, neither was he sad. He always had enough and was thankful for it, for I never yet knew wisdom to go begging or crying.

So he went his way and he fished his fish, and twelve months and a week or more passed by. Then one day he went past the baker shop and there sat Selim the Baker smoking his pipe of tobacco.

'So, friend,' said Selim the Fisherman, 'you are back again in the old place, I see.'

'Yes,' said the other Selim; 'awhile ago I was a king, and now I am nothing but a baker again. As for that gold ring with the red stone—they may say it is Luck's Ring if they choose, but when next I wear it may I be hanged.'

Thereupon he told Selim the Fisherman the story of what had happened to him with all its ins and outs, just as I have told it to you.

'Well!' said Selim the Fisherman, 'I should like to have a sight of that island myself. If you want the ring no longer, just let me have it; for maybe if I wear it something of the kind will happen to me.'

'You may have it,' said Selim the Baker. 'Yonder it is, and you are welcome to it.'

So Selim the Fisherman put on the ring, and then went his way about his own business.

That night, as he came home carrying his nets over his shoulder, whom should he meet but the little old man in grey, with the white beard and the black cap on his head and the long staff in his hand.

'Is your name Selim?' said the little man, just as he had done to Selim the Baker.

'Yes,' said Selim; 'it is.'

'And do you wear a gold ring with a red stone?' said the little old man, just as he had said before.

'Yes,' said Selim; 'I do.'

'Then come with me,' said the little old man, 'and I will show you the wonder of the world.'

Selim the Fisherman remembered all that Selim the Baker had told him, and he took no two thoughts as to what to do. Down he tumbled his nets, and away he went after the other as fast as his legs could carry him. Here they went and there they went, up crooked streets and lanes and down byways and alleyways, until at last they came to the same garden to which Selim the Baker had been brought. Then the old man knocked at the gate three times and cried out in a loud voice, 'Open! Open! Open to Selim who wears the Ring of Luck!'

Then the gate opened, and in they went. Fine as it all was, Selim the Fisherman cared to look neither to the right nor to the left, but straight after the old man he went, until at last they came to the seaside and the boat and the four-and-twenty oarsmen dressed like princes and the black slaves with the perfumed torches. Here the old man entered the boat and Selim after him, and away they sailed.

To make a long story short, everything happened to Selim the Fisherman just as it had happened to Selim the Baker. At dawn of day they came to the island and the city built on the mountain. And the palaces were just as white and beautiful, and the gardens and orchards just as fresh and blooming as though they had not all tumbled down and sunk under the water a week before, almost carrying poor Selim the Baker with them. There were the people dressed in silks and satins and jewels, just as Selim the Baker had found them, and they shouted and hurrahed for Selim the Fisherman just as they had shouted and hurrahed for the other. There were the princes and the nobles and the white horse, and Selim the Fisherman got on his back and rode up to a dazzling snow-white palace, and they put a crown on his head and made a king of him, just as they had made a king of Selim the Baker.

That night, at midnight, it happened just as it had happened before. Suddenly, as the hour struck, the lights all went out, and there was a moaning and a crying enough to make the heart curdle. Then the door flew open, and in came the six terrible black men with torches. They led Selim the Fisherman through damp and dismal entries and passageways until they came to the vaulted room of black marble, and there stood the beautiful statue on its black pedestal. Then came the voice from above—'Selim! Selim! Selim!' it cried, 'what art thou doing? To-day is feasting and drinking and merrymaking, but beware of tomorrow!'

But Selim the Fisherman did not stand still and listen, as Selim the Baker had done. He called out, 'I hear the words! I am listening! I will beware today for the sake of tomorrow!'

I do not know what I should have done had I been king of that island and had I known that in a twelvemonth it would all come tumbling down about my ears and sink into the sea, maybe carry me along with it. This is what Selim the Fisherman did [but then he wore the iron Ring of Wisdom on his finger, and I never had that upon mine]:

First of all, he called the wisest men of the island to him, and found from them just where the other desert island lay upon which the boat with Selim the Baker in it had drifted.

Then, when he had learned where it was to be found, he sent armies and armies of men and built on that island palaces and houses, and planted there orchards and gardens, just like the palaces and the orchards and the gardens about him—only a great deal finer. Then he sent fleets and fleets of ships, and carried everything away from the island where he lived to that other island—all the men and the women and the children; all the flocks and herds and every living thing; all the fowls and the birds and everything that wore feathers; all the gold and the silver and the jewels and the silks and the satins, and whatever was of any good or of any use; and when all these things were done, there were still two days left till the end of the year.

Upon the first of these two days he sent over the beautiful statue and had it set up in the very midst of the splendid new palace he had built.

Upon the second day he went over himself, leaving behind him nothing but the dead mountain and the rocks and the empty houses.

So came the end of the twelve months.

So came midnight.

Out went all the lights in the new palace, and everything was as silent as death and as black as ink. The door opened, and in came the nine men in red, with torches burning as red as blood. They took Selim the Fisherman by the arms and led him to the beautiful statue, and there she was with her eyes open.

'Are you Selim?' said she.

'Yes, I am Selim,' said he.

'And do you wear the iron Ring of Wisdom?' said she.

'Yes, I do,' said he; and so he did.

There was no roaring and thundering, there was no shaking and quaking, there was no toppling and tumbling, there was no splashing and dashing: for this island was solid rock, and was not all enchantment and hollow inside and underneath like the other which he had left behind.

The beautiful statue smiled until the place lit up as though the sun shone. Down she came from the pedestal where she stood and kissed Selim the Fisherman on the lips.

Then instantly the lights blazed everywhere, and the people shouted and cheered, and the music played. But neither Selim the Fisherman nor the beautiful statue saw or heard anything.

'I have done all this for you!' said Selim the Fisherman.

'And I have been waiting for you a thousand years!' said the beautiful statue—only she was not a statue any longer.

After that they were married, and Selim the Fisherman and the enchanted statue became king and queen in real earnest.

I think Selim the Fisherman sent for Selim the Baker and made him rich and happy—I hope he did—I am sure he did.

So, after all, it is not always the lucky one who gathers the plums when wisdom is by to pick up what the other shakes down.

I could say more; for, O little children! little children! there is more than meat in many an egg-shell; and many a fool tells a story that joggles a wise man's wits, and many a man dances and junkets in his fool's paradise till it comes tumbling down about his ears some day; and there are few men who are like Selim the Fisherman, who wear the Ring of Wisdom on their finger, and, alack-a-day! I am not one of them, and that is the end of this story.

5

EMPTY BOTTLES

In the old, old days when men were wiser than they are in these times, there lived a great philosopher and magician, by name Nicholas Flamel. Not only did he know all the actual sciences, but the black arts as well, and magic, and what not. He conjured demons so that when a body passed the house of a moonlight night a body might see imps, great and small, little and big, sitting on the chimney stacks and the ridge pole, clattering their heels on the tiles and chatting together.

He could change iron and lead into silver and gold; he discovered the elixir of life, and might have been living even to this day had he thought it worth while to do so.

There was a student at the university whose name was Gebhart, who was so well acquainted with algebra and geometry that he could tell at a single glance how many drops of water there were in a bottle of wine. As for Latin and Greek—he could patter them off like his A B C's. Nevertheless, he was not satisfied with the things he knew, but was for learning the things that no schools could teach him. So one day he came knocking at Nicholas Flamel's door.

'Come in,' said the wise man, and there Gebhart found him sitting in the midst of his books and bottles and diagrams and dust and chemicals and cobwebs, making strange figures upon the table with jackstraws and a piece of chalk—for your true wise man can squeeze more learning out of jackstraws and a piece of chalk than we common folk can get out of all the books in the world.

No one else was in the room but the wise man's servant, whose name was Babette.

'What is it you want?' said the wise man, looking at Gebhart over the rim of his spectacles.

'Master,' said Gebhart, 'I have studied day after day at the university, and from early in the morning until late at night, so that my head has hummed and my eyes were sore, yet I have not learned those things that I wish most of all to know—the arts that no one but you can teach. Will you take me as your pupil?'

The wise man shook his head.

'Many would like to be as wise as that,' said he, 'and few there be who can become so. Now tell me. Suppose all the riches of the world were offered to you, would you rather be wise?'

'Yes.'

'Suppose you might have all the rank and power of a king or of an emperor, would you rather be wise?'

'Yes.'

'Suppose I undertook to teach you, would you give up everything of joy and of pleasure to follow me?'

'Yes.'

'Perhaps you are hungry,' said the master.

'Yes,' said the student, 'I am.'

'Then, Babette, you may bring some bread and cheese.'

It seemed to Gebhart that he had learned all that Nicholas Flamel had to teach him.

It was in the grey of the dawning, and the master took the pupil by the hand and led him up the rickety stairs to the roof of the house, where nothing was to be seen but grey sky, high roofs, and chimney stacks from which the smoke rose straight into the still air.

'Now,' said the master, 'I have taught you nearly all of the science that I know, and the time has come to show you the wonderful thing that has been waiting for us from the beginning when time was. You have given up wealth and the world and pleasure and joy and love for the sake of wisdom. Now, then, comes the last test—whether you can remain faithful to me to the end; if you fail in it, all is lost that you have gained.'

After he said that he stripped his cloak away from his shoulders and laid bare the skin. Then he took a bottle of red liquor and began bathing his shoulder blades with it; and as Gebhart, squatting upon the ridge pole, looked, he saw two little lumps bud out upon the smooth skin, and then grow and grow and grow until they became two great wings as white as snow.

'Now then,' said the master, 'take me by the belt and grip fast, for there is a long, long journey before us, and if you should lose your head and let go your hold you will fall and be dashed to pieces.'

Then he spread the two great wings, and away he flew as fast as the wind, with Gebhart hanging to his belt.

Over hills, over dales, over mountains, over moors he flew, with the brown earth lying so far below that horses and cows looked like pismires and men like fleas.

Then, by and by, it was over the ocean they were crossing, with the great ships that pitched and tossed below looking like chips in a puddle in rainy weather.

At last they came to a strange land, far, far away, and there the master lit upon a sea shore where the sand was as white as silver. As soon as his feet touched the hard ground the great wings were gone like a puff of smoke, and the wise man walked like any other body.

At the edge of the sandy beach was a great, high, naked

cliff; and the only way of reaching the top was by a flight of stone steps, as slippery as glass, cut in the solid rock.

The wise man led the way, and the student followed close at his heels, every now and then slipping and stumbling so that, had it not been for the help that the master gave him, he would have fallen more than once and have been dashed to pieces upon the rocks below.

At last they reached the top, and there found themselves in a desert, without stick of wood or blade of grass, but only grey stones and skulls and bones bleaching in the sun.

In the middle of the plain was a castle such as the eyes of man never saw before, for it was built all of crystal from roof to cellar. Around it was a high wall of steel, and in the wall were seven gates of polished brass.

The wise man led the way straight to the middle gate of the seven, where there hung a horn of pure silver, which he set to his lips. He blew a blast so loud and shrill that it made Gebhart's ears tingle. In an instant there sounded a great rumble and grumble like the noise of loud thunder, and the gates of brass swung slowly back, as though of themselves.

But when Gebhart saw what he saw within the gates his heart crumbled away for fear, and his knees knocked together; for there, in the very middle of the way, stood a monstrous, hideous dragon, that blew out flames and clouds of smoke from his gaping mouth like a chimney afire.

But the wise master was as cool as smooth water; he thrust his hand into the bosom of his jacket and drew forth a little black box, which he flung straight into the gaping mouth.

Snap!—the dragon swallowed the box.

The next moment it gave a great, loud, terrible cry, and, clapping and rattling its wings, leaped into the air and flew away, bellowing like a bull.

If Gebhart had been wonderstruck at seeing the outside

of the castle, he was ten thousand times more amazed to see the inside thereof. For, as the master led the way and he followed, he passed through four-and-twenty rooms, each one more wonderful than the other. Everywhere was gold and silver and dazzling jewels that glistened so brightly that one had to shut one's eyes to their sparkle. Beside all this, there were silks and satins and velvets and laces and crystal and ebony and sandal-wood that smelled sweeter than musk and rose leaves. All the wealth of the world brought together into one place could not make such riches as Gebhart saw with his two eyes in these four-and-twenty rooms. His heart beat fast within him.

At last they reached a little door of solid iron, beside which hung a sword with a blade that shone like lightning. The master took the sword in one hand and laid the other upon the latch of the door. Then he turned to Gebhart and spoke for the first time since they had started upon their long journey.

'In this room,' said he, 'you will see a strange thing happen, and in a little while I shall be as one dead. As soon as that comes to pass, go you straightway through to the room beyond, where you will find upon a marble table a goblet of water and a silver dagger. Touch nothing else, and look at nothing else, for if you do all will be lost to both of us. Bring the water straightway, and sprinkle my face with it, and when that is done you and I will be the wisest and greatest men that ever lived, for I will make you equal to myself in all that I know. So now swear to do what I have just bid you, and not turn aside a hair's breadth in the going and the coming.

'I swear,' said Gebhart, and crossed his heart.

Then the master opened the door and entered, with Gebhart close at his heels.

In the centre of the room was a great red cock, with eyes that shone like sparks of fire. So soon as he saw the master he flew at him, screaming fearfully, and spitting out darts of fire that blazed and sparkled like lightning.

It was a dreadful battle between the master and the cock. Up and down they fought, and here and there. Sometimes the student could see the wise man whirling and striking with his sword; and then again he would be hidden in a sheet of flame. But after a while he made a lucky stroke, and off flew the cock's head. Then, lo and behold! Instead of a cock it was a great, hairy, black demon that lay dead on the floor.

But, though the master had conquered, he looked like one sorely sick. He was just able to stagger to a couch that stood by the wall, and there he fell and lay, without breath or motion, like one dead, and as white as wax.

As soon as Gebhart had gathered his wits together he remembered what the master had said about the other room.

The door of it was also of iron. He opened it and passed within, and there saw two great tables or blocks of polished marble. Upon one was the dagger and a goblet of gold brimming with water. Upon the other lay the figure of a woman, and as Gebhart looked at her he thought her more beautiful than any thought or dream could picture. But her eyes were closed, and she lay like a lifeless figure of wax.

After Gebhart had gazed at her a long, long time, he took up the goblet and the dagger from the table and turned towards the door.

Then, before he left that place, he thought that he would have just one more look at the beautiful figure. So he did, and gazed and gazed until his heart melted away within him like a lump of butter; and, hardly knowing what he did, he stooped and kissed the lips.

Instantly he did so a great humming sound filled the whole castle, so sweet and musical that it made him tremble to listen. Then suddenly the figure opened its eyes and looked straight at him.

'At last!' she said; 'have you come at last?'

'Yes,' said Gebhart, 'I have come.'

Then the beautiful woman arose and stepped down from the table to the floor; and if Gebhart thought her beautiful before, he thought her a thousand times more beautiful now that her eyes looked into his.

'Listen,' said she. 'I have been asleep for hundreds upon hundreds of years, for so it was fated to be until he should come who was to bring me back to life again. You are he, and now you shall live with me forever. In this castle is the wealth gathered by the king of the genii, and it is greater than all the riches of the world. It and the castle likewise shall be yours. I can transport everything into any part of the world you choose, and can by my arts make you prince or king or emperor. Come.'

'Stop,' said Gebhart. 'I must first do as my master bade me.'

He led the way into the other room, the lady following him, and so they both stood together by the couch where the wise man lay. When the lady saw his face she cried out in a loud voice: 'It is the great master! What are you going to do?'

'I am going to sprinkle his face with this water,' said Gebhart.

'Stop!' said she. 'Listen to what I have to say. In your hand you hold the water of life and the dagger of death. The master is not dead, but sleeping; if you sprinkle that water upon him he will awaken, young, handsome and more powerful than the greatest magician that ever lived. I myself, this castle, and everything that is in it will be his, and, instead of your becoming a prince or a king or an emperor, he will be so in your place. That, I say, will happen if he wakens. Now the dagger of death is the only thing in the world that has power to kill him. You have it in your hand. You have but to give him one stroke with it while he sleeps, and he will never waken again, and then all will be yours—your very own.'

Gebhart neither spoke nor moved, but stood looking down upon his master. Then he set down the goblet very softly on the floor, and, shutting his eyes that he might not see the blow, raised the dagger to strike.

'That is all your promises amount to,' said Nicholas Flamel the wise man. 'After all, Babette, you need not bring the bread and cheese, for he shall be no pupil of mine.'

Then Gebhart opened his eyes.

There sat the wise man in the midst of his books and bottles and diagrams and dust and chemicals and cobwebs, making strange figures upon the table with jackstraws and a piece of chalk.

And Babette, who had just opened the cupboard door for the loaf of bread and the cheese, shut it again with a bang, and went back to her spinning.

So Gebhart had to go back again to his Greek and Latin and algebra and geometry; for, after all, one cannot pour a gallon of beer into a quart pot, or the wisdom of a Nicholas Flamel into such an one as Gebhart.

As for the name of this story, why, if some promises are not bottles full of nothing but wind, there is little need to have a name for anything.

6

THE FRUIT OF HAPPINESS

Once upon a time there was a servant who served a wise man, and cooked for him his cabbage and his onions and his pot-herbs and his broth, day after day, time in and time out, for seven years.

In those years the servant was well enough contented, but no one likes to abide in the same place forever, and so one day he took it into his head that he would like to go out into the world to see what kind of a fortune a man might make there for himself. 'Very well,' says the wise man, the servant's master; 'you have served me faithfully these seven years gone, and now that you ask leave to go you shall go. But it is little or nothing in the way of money that I can give you, and so you will have to be content with what I can afford. See, here is a little pebble, and its like is not to be found in the seven kingdoms, for whoever holds it in his mouth can hear while he does so all that the birds and the beasts say to one another. Take it—it is yours, and, if you use it wisely, it may bring you a fortune.'

The servant would rather have had the money in hand than the magic pebble, but, as nothing better was to be had, he took the little stone, and, bidding his master good-bye, trudged out into the world, to seek his fortune. Well, he jogged on and on, paying his way with the few pennies he had saved in his seven years of service, but for all of his travelling nothing of good happened to him until, one morning, he came to a lonely place where there stood a gallows, and there he sat him down to rest, and it is just in such an unlikely place as this that a man's best chance of fortune comes to him sometimes.

As the servant sat there, there came two ravens flying, and lit upon the cross-beam overhead. There they began talking to one another, and the servant popped the pebble into his mouth to hear what they might say.

'Yonder is a traveller in the world,' said the first raven.

'Yes,' said the second, 'and if he only knew how to set about it, his fortune is as good as made.'

'How is that so?' said the first raven.

'Why, thus,' said the second. 'If he only knew enough to follow yonder road over the hill, he would come by and by to a stone cross where two roads meet, and there he would find a man sitting. If he would ask it of him, that man would lead him to the garden where the fruit of happiness grows.'

'The fruit of happiness!' said the first raven, 'and of what use would the fruit of happiness be to him?'

'What use? I tell you, friend, there is no fruit in the world like that, for one has only to hold it in one's hand and wish, and whatever one asks for one shall have.'

You may guess that when the servant understood the talk of the ravens he was not slow in making use of what he heard. Up he scrambled, and away he went as fast as his legs could carry him. On and on he travelled, until he came to the cross-roads and the stone cross of which the raven spoke, and there, sure enough, sat the traveller. He was clad in a weather-stained coat, and he wore dusty boots, and the servant bade him good-morning.

How should the servant know that it was an angel whom

he beheld, and not a common wayfarer?

'Whither away, comrade,' asked the traveller.

'Out in the world,' said the servant, 'to seek my fortune. And what I want to know is this—will you guide me to where I can find the fruit of happiness?'

'You ask a great thing of me,' said the other; 'nevertheless, since you do ask it, it is not for me to refuse, though I may tell you that many a man has sought for that fruit, and few indeed have found it. But if I guide you to the garden where the fruit grows, there is one condition you must fulfil: many strange things will happen upon our journey between here and there, but concerning all you see you must ask not a question and say not a word. Do you agree to that?'

'Yes,' said the servant, 'I do.'

'Very well,' said his new comrade; 'then let us be jogging, for I have business in the town tonight, and the time is none too long to get there.'

So all the rest of that day they journeyed onward together, until, towards evening, they came to a town with high towers and steep roofs and tall spires. The servant's companion entered the gate as though he knew the place right well, and led the way up one street and down another, until, by and by, they came to a noble house that stood a little apart by itself, with gardens of flowers and fruit trees all around it. There the travelling companion stopped, and, drawing out a little pipe from under his jacket, began playing so sweetly upon it that he made one's heart stand still to listen to the music.

Well, he played and played until, by and by, the door opened, and out came a servingman. 'Ho, piper!' said he, 'would you like to earn good wages for your playing?'

'Yes,' said the travelling companion, 'I would, for that is why I came hither.'

'Then follow me,' said the servant, and thereupon the

travelling companion tucked away his pipe and entered, with the other at his heels.

The house servant led the way from one room to another, each grander than the one they left behind, until at last he came to a great hall where dozens of servants were serving a fine feast. But only one man sat at table—a young man with a face so sorrowful that it made a body's heart ache to look upon him. 'Can you play good music, piper?' said he.

'Yes,' said the piper, 'that I can, for I know a tune that can cure sorrow. But before I blow my pipe, I and my friend here must have something to eat and drink, for one cannot play well with an empty stomach.'

'So be it,' said the young man; 'sit down with me and eat and drink.'

So the two did without second bidding, and such food and drink the servingman had never tasted in his life before. And while they were feasting together the young man told them his story, and why it was he was so sad. A year before he had married a young lady, the most beautiful in all that kingdom, and had friends and comrades and all things that a man could desire in the world. But suddenly everything went wrong; his wife and he fell out and quarrelled until there was no living together, and she had to go back to her old home. Then his companions deserted him, and now he lived all alone.

'Yours is a hard case,' said the travelling companion, 'but it is not past curing.' Thereupon he drew out his pipes and began to play, and it was such a tune as no man ever listened to before. He played and he played, and, after a while, one after another of those who listened to him began to get drowsy. First they winked, then they shut their eyes, and then they nodded until all were as dumb as logs, and as sound asleep as though they would never waken again. Only the servant and the piper stayed awake, for the music did not make them drowsy as it did the rest. Then, when all but they two were tight and fast asleep, the travelling companion arose, tucked away his pipe, and, stepping up to the young man, took from off his finger a splendid ruby ring, as red as blood and as bright as fire, and popped the same into his pocket. And all the while the servingman stood gaping like a fish to see what his comrade was about. 'Come,' said the travelling companion, 'it is time we were going,' and off they went, shutting the door behind them.

As for the servingman, though he remembered his promise and said nothing concerning what he had beheld, his wits buzzed in his head like a hive of bees, for he thought that of all the ugly tricks he had seen, none was more ugly than this—to bewitch the poor sorrowful young man into a sleep, and then to rob him of his ruby ring after he had fed them so well and had treated them so kindly.

But the next day they jogged on together again until by and by they came to a great forest. There they wandered up and down till night came upon them and found them still stumbling onward through the darkness, while the poor servingman's flesh quaked to hear the wild beasts and the wolves growling and howling around them.

But all the while the angel—his travelling companion—said never a word; he seemed to doubt nothing nor fear nothing, but trudged straight ahead until, by and by, they saw a light twinkling far away, and, when they came to it, they found a gloomy stone house, as ugly as eyes ever looked upon. Up stepped the servant's comrade and knocked upon the door— rap! tap! tap! By and by it was opened a crack, and there stood an ugly old woman, blear-eyed and crooked and gnarled as a winter twig. But the heart within her was good for all that. 'Alas, poor folk!' she cried, 'why do you come here? This is a den where lives a band of wicked thieves. Every day they go out to rob and murder poor travellers like yourselves. By and by they will come back, and when they find you here they will certainly kill you.'

'No matter for that,' said the travelling companion; 'we can go no farther tonight, so you must let us in and hide us as best you may.'

And in he went, as he said, with the servant at his heels trembling like a leaf at what he had heard. The old woman gave them some bread and meat to eat, and then hid them away in the great empty meal-chest in the corner, and there they lay as still as mice.

By and by in came the gang of thieves with a great noise and uproar, and down they sat to their supper. The poor servant lay in the chest listening to all they said of the dreadful things they had done that day—how they had cruelly robbed and murdered poor people. Every word that they said he heard, and he trembled until his teeth chattered in his head. But all the same the robbers knew nothing of the two being there, and there they lay until near the dawning of the day. Then the travelling companion bade the servant be stirring, and up they got, and out of the chest they came, and found all the robbers sound asleep and snoring so that the dust flew.

'Stop a bit,' said the angel—the travelling companion—'we must pay them for our lodging.'

As he spoke he drew from his pocket the ruby ring which he had stolen from the sorrowful young man's finger, and dropped it into the cup from which the robber captain drank. Then he led the way out of the house, and, if the servingman had wondered the day before at that which the comrade did, he wondered ten times more to see him give so beautiful a ring to such wicked and bloody thieves.

The third evening of their journey the two travellers came to a little hut, neat enough, but as poor as poverty, and there the comrade knocked upon the door and asked for lodging. In the house lived a poor man and his wife; and, though the two were as honest as the palm of your hand, and as good and kind as rain in springtime, they could hardly scrape enough of a living to keep body and soul together. Nevertheless, they made the travellers welcome, and set before them the very best that was to be had in the house; and, after both had eaten and drunk, they showed them to bed in a corner as clean as snow, and there they slept the night through.

But the next morning, before the dawning of the day, the travelling companion was stirring again. 'Come,' said he; 'rouse yourself, for I have a bit of work to do before I leave this place.'

And strange work it was! When they had come outside of the house, he gathered together a great heap of straw and sticks of wood, and stuffed all under the corner of the house. Then he struck a light and set fire to it, and, as the two walked away through the grey dawn, all was a red blaze behind them.

Still, the servant remembered his promise to his travelling comrade, and said never a word or asked never a question, though all that day he walked on the other side of the road, and would have nothing to say or to do with the other. But never a whit did his comrade seem to think of or to care for that. On they jogged, and, by the time evening was at hand, they had come to a neat cottage with apple and pear trees around it, all as pleasant as the eye could desire to see. In this cottage lived a widow and her only son, and they also made the travellers welcome, and set before them a good supper and showed them to a clean bed.

This time the travelling comrade did neither good nor ill to those of the house, but in the morning he told the widow whither they were going, and asked if she and her son knew the way to the garden where grew the fruit of happiness.

'Yes,' said she, 'that we do, for the garden is not a day's journey from here, and my son himself shall go with you to show you the way.'

'That is good,' said the servant's comrade, 'and if he will do so I will pay him well for his trouble.'

So the young man put on his hat, and took up his stick, and off went the three, up hill and down dale, until by and by they came over the top of the last hill, and there below them lay the garden.

And what a sight it was, the leaves shining and glistening like so many jewels in the sunlight! I only wish that I could tell you how beautiful that garden was. And in the middle of it grew a golden tree, and on it golden fruit. The servant, who had travelled so long and so far, could see it plainly from where he stood, and he did not need to be told that it was the fruit of happiness. But, after all, all he could do was to stand and look, for in front of them was a great raging torrent, without a bridge for a body to cross over.

'Yonder is what you seek,' said the young man, pointing with his finger, 'and there you can see for yourself the fruit of happiness.'

The travelling companion said never a word, good or bad, but, suddenly catching the widow's son by the collar, he lifted him and flung him into the black, rushing water. Splash! went the young man, and then away he went whirling over rocks and waterfalls. 'There!' cried the comrade, 'that is your reward for your service!'

When the servant saw this cruel, wicked deed, he found his tongue at last, and all that he had bottled up for the seven days came frothing out of him like hot beer. Such abuse as he showered upon his travelling companion no man ever listened to before. But to all the servant said the other answered never a word until he had stopped for sheer want of breath. Then—

'Poor fool,' said the travelling companion, 'if you had only held your tongue a minute longer, you, too, would have had the fruit of happiness in your hand. Now it will be many a day before you have a sight of it again.'

Thereupon, as he ended speaking, he struck his staff upon the ground. Instantly the earth trembled, and the sky darkened overhead until it grew as black as night. Then came a great flash of fire from up in the sky, which wrapped the travelling companion about until he was hidden from sight. Then the flaming fire flew away to heaven again, carrying him along with it. After that the sky cleared once more, and, lo and behold! The garden and the torrent and all were gone, and nothing was left but a naked plain covered over with the bones of those who had come that way before, seeking the fruit which the travelling servant had sought.

It was a long time before the servant found his way back into the world again, and the first house he came to, weak and hungry, was the widow's.

But what a change he beheld! It was a poor cottage no longer, but a splendid palace, fit for a queen to dwell in. The widow herself met him at the door, and she was dressed in clothes fit for a queen to wear, shining with gold and silver and precious stones.

The servant stood and stared like one bereft of wits. 'How comes all this change?' said he, 'and how did you get all these grand things?'

'My son,' said the widow woman, 'has just been to the garden, and has brought home from there the fruit of happiness. Many a day did we search, but never could we find how to enter into the garden, until, the other day, an angel came and showed the way to my son, and he was able not only to gather of the fruit for himself, but to bring an apple for me also.'

Then the poor travelling servant began to thump his head. He saw well enough through the millstone now, and that he, too, might have had one of the fruit if he had but held his tongue a little longer.

Yes, he saw what a fool he had made of himself, when he learned that it was an angel with whom he had been travelling the five days gone.

But, then, we are all of us like the servant for the matter of that; I, too, have travelled with an angel many a day, I dare say, and never knew it.

That night the servant lodged with the widow and her son, and the next day he started back home again upon the way he had travelled before. By evening, he had reached the place where the house of the poor couple stood—the house that he had seen the angel set fire to. There he beheld masons and carpenters hard at work hacking and hewing, and building a fine new house. And there he saw the poor man himself standing by giving them orders. 'How is this,' said the travelling servant; 'I thought that your house was burned down?'

'So it was, and that is how I came to be rich now,' said the one-time poor man. 'I and my wife had lived in our old house for many a long day, and never knew that a great treasure of silver and gold was hidden beneath it, until a few days ago there came an angel and burned it down over our heads, and in the morning we found the treasure. So now we are rich for as long as we may live.'

The next morning, the poor servant jogged along on his homeward way more sad and downcast than ever, and by evening he had come to the robbers' den in the thick woods, and there the old woman came running to the door to meet him. 'Come in!' cried she; 'come in and welcome! The robbers are all dead and gone now, and I use the treasure that they left behind to entertain poor travellers like yourself. The other day there came an angel hither, and with him he brought the ring of discord that breeds spite and rage and quarrelling. He gave it to the captain of the band, and after he had gone the robbers fought for it with one another until they were all killed. So now the world is rid of them, and travellers can come and go as they please.'

Back jogged the travelling servant, and the next day came to the town and to the house of the sorrowful young man. There, lo and behold! Instead of being dark and silent, as it was before, all was ablaze with light, and noisy with the sound of rejoicing and merriment. There happened to be one of the household standing at the door, and he knew the servant as the companion of that one who had stolen the ruby ring. Up he came and laid hold of the servant by the collar, calling to his companions that he had caught one of the thieves. Into the house they hauled the poor servant, and into the same room where he had been before, and there sat the young man at a grand feast, with his wife and all his friends around him. But when the young man saw the poor servingman he came to him and took him by the hand, and set him beside himself at the table. 'Nobody except your comrade could be so welcome as you,' said he, 'and this is why. An enemy of mine one time gave me a ruby ring, and though I knew nothing of it, it was the ring of discord that bred strife wherever it came. So, as soon as it was brought into the house, my wife and all my friends fell out with me, and we quarrelled so that they all left me. But, though I knew it not at that time, your comrade was an angel, and took the ring away with him, and now I am as happy as I was sorrowful before.'

By the next night the servant had come back to his home again. Rap! tap! tap! He knocked at the door, and the wise man who had been his master opened to him. 'What do you want?' said he.

'I want to take service with you again,' said the travelling servant.

'Very well,' said the wise man; 'come in and shut the door.'

And for all I know the travelling servant is there to this day. For he is not the only one in the world who has come in sight of the fruit of happiness, and then jogged all the way back home again to cook cabbage and onions and pot-herbs, and to make broth for wiser men than himself to sup.

That is the end of this story.

7

ILL-LUCK AND THE FIDDLER

Once upon a time St Nicholas came down into the world to take a peep at the old place and see how things looked in the spring-time. On he stepped along the road to the town where he used to live, for he had a notion to find out whether things were going on nowadays as they one time did. By and by he came to a cross-road, and who should he see sitting there but Ill-Luck himself. Ill-Luck's face was as grey as ashes, and his hair as white as snow—for he is as old as Grandfather Adam—and two great wings grew out of his shoulders—for he flies fast and comes quickly to those whom he visits, does Ill-Luck.

Now, St Nicholas had a pocketful of hazelnuts, which he kept cracking and eating as he trudged along the road, and just then he came upon one with a worm-hole in it. When he saw Ill-Luck it came into his head to do a good turn to poor sorrowful man.

'Good-morning, Ill-Luck,' says he.

'Good-morning, St Nicholas,' says Ill-Luck.

'You look as hale and strong as ever,' says St Nicholas.

'Ah, yes,' says Ill-Luck, 'I find plenty to do in this world of woe.'

'They tell me,' says St Nicholas, 'that you can go wherever you choose, even if it be through a keyhole; now, is that so?'

'Yes,' says Ill-Luck, 'it is.'

'Well, look now, friend,' says St Nicholas, 'could you go into this hazelnut if you chose to?'

'Yes,' says Ill-Luck, 'I could indeed.'

'I should like to see you,' says St Nicholas; 'for then I should be of a mind to believe what people say of you.'

'Well,' says Ill-Luck, 'I have not much time to be pottering and playing upon Jack's fiddle; but to oblige an old friend'—thereupon he made himself small and smaller, and—phst! he was in the nut before you could wink.

Then what do you think St Nicholas did? In his hand he held a little plug of wood, and no sooner had Ill-Luck entered the nut than he stuck the plug in the hole, and there was man's enemy as tight as fly in a bottle.

'So!' says St Nicholas, 'that's a piece of work well done.' Then he tossed the hazelnut under the roots of an oak tree near by, and went his way.

And that is how this story begins.

Well, the hazelnut lay and lay and lay, and all the time that it lay there nobody met with ill-luck; but, one day, who should come travelling that way but a rogue of a Fiddler, with his fiddle under his arm. The day was warm, and he was tired; so down he sat under the shade of the oak tree to rest his legs. By and by he heard a little shrill voice piping and crying, 'Let me out! let me out! let me out!'

The Fiddler looked up and down, but he could see nobody. 'Who are you?' says he.

'I am Ill-Luck! Let me out! let me out!'

'Let you out?' says the Fiddler. 'Not I. If you are bottled up here it is the better for all of us.' And, so saying, he tucked his fiddle under his arm and off he marched.

But before he had gone six steps he stopped. He was one of your peering, prying sort, and liked more than a little to know all that was to be known about this or that or the other thing that he chanced to see or hear. 'I wonder where Ill-Luck can be, to be in such a tight place as he seems to be caught in,' says he to himself; and back he came again. 'Where are you, Ill-Luck?' says he.

'Here I am,' says Ill-Luck, 'here in this hazelnut, under the roots of the oak tree.'

Thereupon the Fiddler laid aside his fiddle and bow, and fell to poking and prying under the roots until he found the nut. Then he began twisting and turning it in his fingers, looking first on one side and then on the other, and all the while Ill-Luck kept crying, 'Let me out! let me out!'

It was not long before the Fiddler found the little wooden plug, and then nothing he would do but he must take a peep inside the nut to see if Ill-Luck was really there. So he picked and pulled at the wooden plug, until at last out it came; and—phst! pop! Out came Ill-Luck along with it.

Plague take the Fiddler! say I.

'Listen,' says Ill-Luck. 'It has been many a long day that I have been in that hazelnut, and you are the man that has let me out; for once in a way I will do a good turn to a poor human body.' Therewith, and without giving the Fiddler time to speak a word, Ill-Luck caught him up by the belt, and—whiz! Away he flew like a bullet, over hill and over valley; over moor and over mountain, so fast that not enough wind was left in the Fiddler's stomach to say 'Bo!'

By and by he came to a garden, and there he let the Fiddler drop on the soft grass below. Then away he flew to attend to other matters of greater need.

When the Fiddler had gathered his wits together, and himself to his feet, he saw that he lay in a beautiful garden of flowers and fruit trees and marble walks and what not, and that at the end of it stood a great, splendid house, all built of white marble, with a fountain in front, and peacocks strutting about on the lawn.

Well, the Fiddler smoothed down his hair and brushed his clothes a bit, and off he went to see what was to be seen at the grand house at the end of the garden.

He entered the door, and nobody said no to him. Then he passed through one room after another, and each was finer than the one he left behind. Many servants stood around; but they only bowed, and never asked whence he came. At last he came to a room where a little old man sat at a table. The table was spread with a feast that smelled so good that it brought tears to the Fiddler's eyes and water to his mouth, and all the plates were of pure gold. The little old man sat alone, but another place was spread, as though he were expecting some one. As the Fiddler came in, the little old man nodded and smiled. 'Welcome!' he cried; 'and have you come at last?'

'Yes,' said the Fiddler, 'I have. It was Ill-Luck that brought me.'

'Nay,' said the little old man, 'do not say that. Sit down to the table and eat; and when I have told you all, you will say it was not Ill-Luck, but Good-Luck, that brought you.'

The Fiddler had his own mind about that; but, all the same, down he sat at the table, and fell to with knife and fork at the good things, as though he had not had a bite to eat for a week of Sundays.

'I am the richest man in the world,' says the little old man, after a while.

'I am glad to hear it,' says the Fiddler.

'You may well be,' said the old man, 'for I am all alone in the world, and without wife or child. And this morning I said to myself that the first body that came to my house I would take for a son—or a daughter, as the case might be. You are the first, and so you shall live with me as long as I live, and after I am gone everything that I have shall be yours.'

The Fiddler did nothing but stare with open eyes and mouth, as though he would never shut either again.

Well, the Fiddler lived with the old man for maybe three or four days as snug and happy a life as ever a mouse passed in a green cheese. As for the gold and silver and jewels—why, they were as plentiful in that house as dust in a mill! Everything the Fiddler wanted came to his hand. He lived high, and slept soft and warm, and never knew what it was to want either more or less, or great or small. In all of those three or four days he did nothing but enjoy himself with might and main.

But by and by he began to wonder where all the good things came from. Then, before long, he fell to pestering the old man with questions about the matter.

At first the old man put him off with short answers, but the Fiddler was a master hand at finding out anything he wanted to know. He dinned and drummed and worried until flesh and blood could stand it no longer. So at last the old man said that he would show him the treasure house where all his wealth came from, and at that the Fiddler was tickled beyond measure.

The old man took a key from behind the door and led him out into the garden. There in a corner by the wall was a great trapdoor of iron. The old man fitted the key to the lock and turned it. He lifted the door, and then went down a steep flight of stone steps, and the Fiddler followed close at his heels. Down below it was as light as day, for in the centre of the room hung a great lamp that shone with a bright light and lit up all the place as bright as day. In the floor were set three great basins of marble: one was nearly full of silver, one of gold and one of gems of all sorts.

'All this is mine,' said the old man, 'and after I am gone it shall be yours. It was left to me as I will leave it to you, and in the meantime you may come and go as you choose and fill your pockets whenever you wish to. But there is one thing you must not do: you must never open that door yonder at the back of the room. Should you do so, Ill-Luck will be sure to overtake you.'

Oh no! The Fiddler would never think of doing such a thing as opening the door. The silver and gold and jewels were enough for him. But since the old man had given him leave, he would just help himself to a few of the fine things. So he stuffed his pockets full, and then he followed the old man up the steps and out into the sunlight again.

It took him maybe an hour to count all the money and jewels he had brought up with him. After he had done that, he began to wonder what was inside of the little door at the back of the room. First he wondered; then he began to grow curious; then he began to itch and tingle and burn as though fifty thousand I-want-to-know nettles were sticking into him from top to toe. At last he could stand it no longer. 'I'll just go down yonder,' says he, 'and peep through the keyhole; perhaps I can see what is there without opening the door.'

So down he took the key, and off he marched to the garden. He opened the trapdoor, and went down the steep steps to the room below. There was the door at the end of the room, but when he came to look there was no keyhole to it. 'Pshaw!' said he, 'here is a pretty state of affairs. Tut! tut! tut! Well, since I have come so far, it would be a pity to turn back without seeing more.' So he opened the door and peeped in.

'Pooh!' said the Fiddler, 'There's nothing there, after all,' and he opened the door wide.

Before him was a great long passageway, and at the far end of it he could see a spark of light as though the sun were shining there. He listened, and after a while he heard a sound like the waves beating on the shore. 'Well,' says he, 'this is the most curious thing I have seen for a long time. Since I have come so far, I may as well see the end of it.' So he entered the passageway, and closed the door behind him. He went on and on, and the spark of light kept growing larger and larger, and by and by—pop! out he came at the other end of the passage.

Sure enough, there he stood on the sea shore, with the waves beating and dashing on the rocks. He stood looking and wondering to find himself in such a place, when all of a sudden something came with a whiz and a rush and caught him by the belt, and away he flew like a bullet.

By and by he managed to screw his head around and look up, and there it was Ill-Luck that had him. 'I thought so,' said the Fiddler; and then he gave over kicking.

Well; on and on they flew, over hill and valley, over moor and mountain, until they came to another garden, and there Ill-Luck let the Fiddler drop.

Swash! Down he fell into the top of an apple tree, and there he hung in the branches.

It was the garden of a royal castle, and all had been weeping and woe (though they were beginning now to pick up their smiles again), and this was the reason why:

The king of that country had died, and no one was left behind him but the queen. But she was a prize, for not only was the kingdom hers, but she was as young as a spring apple and as pretty as a picture; so that there was no end of those who would have liked to have had her, each man for his own. Even that day there were three princes at the castle, each one wanting the queen to marry him; and the wrangling and bickering and squabbling that was going on was enough to deafen a body. The poor young queen was tired to death with it all, and so she had come out into the garden for a bit of rest; and there she sat under the shade of an apple tree, fanning herself and crying, when—

Swash! Down fell the Fiddler into the apple tree and down

fell a dozen apples, popping and tumbling about the queen's ears.

The queen looked up and screamed, and the Fiddler climbed down.

'Where did you come from?' said she.

'Oh, Ill-Luck brought me,' said the Fiddler.

'Nay,' said the queen, 'do not say so. You fell from heaven, for I saw it with my eyes and heard it with my ears. I see how it is now. You were sent hither from heaven to be my husband, and my husband you shall be. You shall be king of this country, half-and-half with me as queen, and shall sit on a throne beside me.'

You can guess whether or not that was music to the Fiddler's ears.

So the princes were sent packing, and the Fiddler was married to the queen, and reigned in that country.

Well, three or four days passed, and all was as sweet and happy as a spring day. But at the end of that time the Fiddler began to wonder what was to be seen in the castle. The queen was very fond of him, and was glad enough to show him all the fine things that were to be seen; so hand in hand they went everywhere, from garret to cellar.

But you should have seen how splendid it all was! The Fiddler felt more certain than ever that it was better to be a king than to be the richest man in the world, and he was as glad as glad could be that Ill-Luck had brought him from the rich little old man over yonder to this.

So he saw everything in the castle but one thing. 'What is behind that door?' said he.

'Ah! that,' said the queen, 'you must not ask or wish to know. Should you open that door Ill-Luck will be sure to overtake you.'

'Pooh!' said the Fiddler, 'I don't care to know, anyhow,' and off they went, hand in hand.

Yes, that was a very fine thing to say; but before an hour had gone by, the Fiddler's head began to hum and buzz like a beehive. 'I don't believe,' said he, 'there would be a grain of harm in my peeping inside that door; all the same, I will not do it. I will just go down and peep through the keyhole.' So off he went to do as he said; but there was no keyhole to that door, either. 'Why, look!' says he, 'it is just like the door at the rich man's house over yonder; I wonder if it is the same inside as outside,' and he opened the door and peeped in. Yes; there was the long passage and the spark of light at the far end, as though the sun were shining. He cocked his head to one side and listened. 'Yes,' said he, 'I think I hear the water rushing, but I am not sure; I will just go a little further in and listen,' and so he entered and closed the door behind him. Well, he went on and on until—pop! there he was out at the farther end, and before he knew what he was about he had stepped out upon the sea shore, just as he had done before.

Whiz! Whirr! Away flew the Fiddler like a bullet, and there was Ill-Luck carrying him by the belt again. Away they sped, over hill and valley, over moor and mountain, until the Fiddler's head grew so dizzy that he had to shut his eyes. Suddenly Ill-Luck let him drop, and down he fell—thump! bump!—on the hard ground. Then he opened his eyes and sat up, and, lo and behold! There he was, under the oak tree whence he had started in the first place. There lay his fiddle, just as he had left it. He picked it up and ran his fingers over the strings—trum, twang! Then he got to his feet and brushed the dirt and grass from his knees. He tucked his fiddle under his arm, and off he stepped upon the way he had been going at first.

'Just to think!' said he, 'I would either have been the richest man in the world, or else I would have been a king, if it had not been for Ill-Luck.'

And that is the way we all of us talk.

8

LITTLE SNOWDROP

Once upon a time, in the middle of winter, when the flakes of snow fell like feathers from the sky, a queen sat at a window set in an ebony frame, and sewed. While she was sewing and watching the snow fall, she pricked her finger with her needle, and three drops of blood dropped on the snow. And because the crimson looked so beautiful on the white snow, she thought: 'Oh that I had a child as white as snow, as red as blood, and as black as the wood of this ebony frame!'

Soon afterwards she had a little daughter, who was as white as snow, as red as blood, and had hair as black as ebony. And when the child was born the queen died.

After a year had gone by the king took another wife. She was a handsome lady, but proud and haughty, and could not endure that any one should surpass her in beauty. She had a wonderful mirror, and whenever she walked up to it, and looked at herself in it, she said:

'Little glass upon the wall,
Who is fairest among us all?'

Then the mirror replied:

'Lady queen, so grand and tall,
Thou art the fairest of them all.'

And she was satisfied, for she knew the mirror always told

the truth. But Snowdrop grew ever taller and fairer, and at seven years old was beautiful as the day, and more beautiful than the queen herself. So once, when the queen asked of her mirror:

'Little glass upon the wall,
Who is fairest among us all?'

It answered:

'Lady queen, you are grand and tall,
But Snowdrop is fairest of you all.'

Then the queen was startled, and turned yellow and green with envy. From that hour she so hated Snowdrop, that she burned with secret wrath whenever she saw the maiden. Pride and envy grew apace like weeds in her heart, till she had no rest day or night. So she called a huntsman and said: 'Take the child out in the forest, for I will endure her no longer in my sight. Kill her, and bring me her lungs and liver as tokens that you have done it.'

The huntsman obeyed, and led the child away; but when he had drawn his hunting knife, and was about to pierce Snowdrop's innocent heart, she began to weep, and said: 'Ah! dear huntsman, spare my life, and I will run deep into the wild forest, and never more come home.'

The huntsman took pity on her, because she looked so lovely, and said, 'Run away then, poor child!' ('The wild beasts will soon make an end of thee,' he thought.) But it seemed as if a stone had been rolled from his heart because he had avoided taking her life; and as a little bear came by just then, he killed it, took out its liver and lungs, and carried them as tokens to the queen. She made the cook dress them with salt, and then the wicked woman ate them, and thought she had eaten Snowdrop's lungs and liver. The poor child was now all alone in the great forest, and she felt frightened as she looked at all the leafy trees, and knew not what to do. So she began to run, and ran over the sharp stones, and through the thorns;

and the wild beasts passed close to her, but did her no harm. She ran as long as her feet could carry her, and when evening closed in, she saw a little house, and went into it to rest herself. Everything in the house was very small, but I cannot tell you how pretty and clean it was.

There stood a little table, covered with a white tablecloth, on which were seven little plates (each little plate with its own little spoon)—also seven little knives and forks, and seven little cups. Round the walls stood seven little beds close together, with sheets as white as snow. Snowdrop being so hungry and thirsty, ate a little of the vegetables and bread on each plate, and drank a drop of wine from every cup, for she did not like to empty one entirely.

Then, being very tired, she laid herself down in one of the beds, but could not make herself comfortable, for one was too long, and another too short. The seventh, luckily, was just right; so there she stayed, said her prayers, and fell asleep.

When it was grown quite dark, home came the masters of the house, seven dwarfs, who delved and mined for iron among the mountains. They lighted their seven candles, and as soon as there was a light in the kitchen, they saw that someone had been there, for it was not quite so orderly as they had left it.

The first said, 'Who has been sitting on my stool?'

The second, 'Who has eaten off my plate?'

The third, 'Who has taken part of my loaf?'

The fourth, 'Who has touched my vegetables?'

The fifth, 'Who has used my fork?'

The sixth, 'Who has cut with my knife?'

The seventh, 'Who has drunk out of my little cup?'

Then the first dwarf looked about, and saw that there was a slight hollow in his bed, so he asked, 'Who has been lying in my little bed?'

The others came running, and each called out, 'Someone

has also been lying in my bed.'

But the seventh, when he looked in his bed, saw Snowdrop there, fast asleep. He called the others, who flocked round with cries of surprise, fetched their seven candles, and cast the light on Snowdrop.

'Oh, heaven,' they cried, 'what a lovely child!' and were so pleased that they would not wake her, but let her sleep on in the little bed. The seventh dwarf slept with all his companions in turn, an hour with each, and so they spent the night. When it was morning Snowdrop woke up, and was frightened when she saw the seven dwarfs. They were very friendly, however, and inquired her name.

'Snowdrop,' answered she.

'How have you found your way to our house?' further asked the dwarfs.

So she told them how her stepmother had tried to kill her, how the huntsman had spared her life, and how she had run the whole day through, till at last she had found their little house.

Then the dwarfs said, 'If thou wilt keep our house, cook, make the beds, wash, sew and knit, and make all neat and clean, thou canst stay with us and shalt want for nothing.'

'I will, right willingly,' said Snowdrop. So she dwelt with them, and kept their house in order. Every morning they went out among the mountains, to seek iron and gold, and came home ready for supper in the evening.

The maiden being left alone all day long, the good dwarfs warned her, saying, 'Beware of thy wicked stepmother, who will soon find out that thou art here; take care that thou lettest nobody in.'

The queen, however, after having, as she thought, eaten Snowdrop's lungs and liver, had no doubt that she was again the first and fairest woman in the world; so she walked up to her mirror, and said:

'Little glass upon the wall,
Who is fairest among us all?'
The mirror replied:
'Lady queen, so grand and tall,
Here you are fairest of them all;
But over the hills, with the seven dwarfs old,
Lives Snowdrop, fairer a hundredfold.'

She trembled, knowing that the mirror never told a falsehood; she felt sure that the huntsman had deceived her, and that Snowdrop was still alive. She pondered once more, late and early, early and late, how best to kill Snowdrop; for envy gave her no rest, day or night, while she herself was not the fairest lady in the land. When she had planned what to do she painted her face, dressed herself like an old pedlar woman, and altered her appearance so much that no one could have known her. In this disguise she went over the seven hills to where the seven dwarfs dwelt, knocked at the door, and cried, 'Good wares, cheap!—very cheap!'

Snowdrop looked out of the window and cried, 'Good-morning, good woman. What have you to sell?'

'Good wares, smart wares,' answered the queen—'bodice laces of all colors;' and drew out one which was woven of colored silk.

'I may surely let this honest dame in!' thought Snowdrop; so she unfastened the door, and bought for herself the pretty lace.

'Child,' said the old woman, 'what a figure thou art! Let me lace thee for once, properly.' Snowdrop feared no harm, so stepped in front of her, and allowed her bodice to be fastened up with the new lace.

But the old woman laced so quick and laced so tight that Snowdrop's breath was stopped, and she fell down as if dead. 'Now I am fairest at last,' said the old woman to herself, and sped away.

The seven dwarfs came home soon after, at eventide, but how alarmed were they to find their poor Snowdrop lifeless on the ground! They lifted her up, and, seeing that she was laced too tightly, cut the lace of her bodice; she began to breathe faintly, and slowly returned to life. When the dwarfs heard what had happened, they said, 'The old pedlar woman was none other than the wicked queen. Be careful of thyself, and open the door to no one if we are not at home.'

The cruel stepmother walked up to her mirror when she reached home, and said:

'Little glass upon the wall,
Who is fairest among us all?'

To which it answered, as usual:

'Lady queen, so grand and tall,
Here you are fairest of them all;
But over the hills, with the seven dwarfs old,
Lives Snowdrop, fairer a hundredfold.'

When she heard this she was so alarmed that all the blood rushed to her heart, for she saw plainly that Snowdrop was still alive.

'This time,' said she, 'I will think of some means that shall destroy her utterly;' and with the help of witchcraft, in which she was skilful, she made a poisoned comb. Then she changed her dress and took the shape of another old woman.

Again she crossed the seven hills to the home of the seven dwarfs, knocked at the door, and cried, 'Good wares, very cheap!'

Snowdrop looked out and said, 'Go away—I dare let no one in.'

'You may surely be allowed to look!' answered the old woman, and she drew out the poisoned comb and held it up. The girl was so pleased with it that she let herself be cajoled, and opened the door.

When the bargain was struck the dame said, 'Now let me dress your hair properly for once.' Poor Snowdrop took no heed, and let the old woman begin; but the comb had scarcely touched her hair before the poison worked, and she fell down senseless.

'Paragon of beauty!' said the wicked woman, 'all is over with thee now,' and went away.

Luckily it was near evening, and the seven dwarfs soon came home. When they found Snowdrop lifeless on the ground they at once distrusted her stepmother. They searched, and found the poisoned comb; and as soon as they had drawn it out, Snowdrop came to herself, and told them what had happened. Again they warned her to be careful, and open the door to no one.

The queen placed herself before the mirror at home and said:

'Little glass upon the wall,
Who is fairest among us all?'

But it again answered:

'Lady queen, so grand and tall,
Here, you are fairest of them all;
But over the hills, with the seven dwarfs old,
Lives Snowdrop, fairer a thousandfold.'

When she heard the mirror speak thus she quivered with rage. 'Snowdrop shall die,' she cried, 'if it costs my own life!'

Then she went to a secret and lonely chamber, where no one ever disturbed her, and compounded an apple of deadly poison. Ripe and rosy cheeked, it was so beautiful to look upon that all who saw it longed for it; but it brought death to any who should eat it. When the apple was ready she painted her face, disguised herself as a peasant woman, and journeyed over the seven hills to where the seven dwarfs dwelt. At the sound of the knock Snowdrop put her head out of the window, and said, 'I cannot open the door to anybody, for the seven dwarfs have forbidden me to do so.'

'Very well,' replied the peasant woman; 'I only want to be rid of my apples. Here, I will give you one of them!'

'No,' said Snowdrop, 'I dare not take it.'

'Art thou afraid of being poisoned?' asked the old woman. 'Look here; I will cut the apple in two, and you shall eat the rosy side, and I the white.'

Now the fruit was so cunningly made that only the rosy side was poisoned. Snowdrop longed for the pretty apple; and when she saw the peasant woman eating it she could resist no longer, but stretched out her hand and took the poisoned half. She had scarcely tasted it when she fell lifeless to the ground.

The queen, laughing loudly, watched her with a barbarous look, and cried: 'Oh, thou who art white as snow, red as blood, and black as ebony, the seven dwarfs cannot awaken thee this time!'

And when she asked the mirror at home,
'Little glass upon the wall,
Who is fairest among us all?'
the mirror at last replied,
'Lady queen, so grand and tall.
You are the fairest of them all.'

So her envious heart had as much repose as an envious heart can ever know.

When the dwarfs came home in the evening they found Snowdrop lying breathless and motionless on the ground. They lifted her up, searched whether she had anything poisonous about her, unlaced her, combed her hair, washed her with water and with wine; but all was useless, for they could not bring the darling back to life. They laid her on a bier, and all the seven placed themselves round it, and mourned for her three long days. Then they would have buried her, but that she still looked so fresh and lifelike, and had such lovely rosy cheeks. 'We cannot lower her into the dark earth,' said they; and caused a transparent coffin of glass to be made, so that she could be seen on all sides, and laid her in it, writing her name outside in letters of gold, which told that she was the daughter of a king. Then they placed the coffin on the mountain above, and one of them always stayed by it and guarded it. But there was little need to guard it, for even the wild animals came and mourned for Snowdrop: the birds likewise—first an owl, and then a raven, and afterwards a dove.

Long, long years did Snowdrop lay in her coffin unchanged, looking as though asleep, for she was still white as snow, red as blood, and her hair was as black as ebony. At last the son of a king chanced to wander into the forest, and came to the dwarf's house for a night's shelter. He saw the coffin on the mountain with the beautiful Snowdrop in it, and read what was written there in letters of gold. Then he said to the dwarfs, 'Let me have the coffin! I will give you whatever you like to ask for it.'

But the dwarfs answered, 'We would not part with it for all the gold in the world.'

He said again, 'Yet give it me; for I cannot live without seeing Snowdrop, and though she is dead, I will prize and honor her as my beloved.'

Then the good dwarfs took pity on him, and gave him the coffin. The prince had it borne away by his servants. They happened to stumble over a bush, and the shock forced the bit of poisoned apple which Snowdrop had tasted out of her throat. Immediately she opened her eyes, raised the coffin lid, and sat up alive once more. 'Oh, heaven!' cried she, 'where am I?'

The prince answered, joyfully. 'Thou art with me,' and told her what had happened, saying, 'I love thee more dearly than anything else in the world. Come with me to my father's castle, and be my wife.'

Snowdrop, well pleased, went with him, and they were married with much state and grandeur.

The wicked stepmother was invited to the feast. Richly dressed, she stood before the mirror, and asked of it:

'Little glass upon the wall,
Who is fairest among us all?'

The mirror answered:

'Lady queen, so grand and tall,
Here, you are fairest among them all;
But the young queen over the mountains old
Is fairer than you a thousand fold.'

The evil-hearted woman uttered a curse, and could scarcely endure her anguish. She first resolved not to attend the wedding, but curiosity would not allow her to rest. She determined to travel, and see who that young queen could be, who was the most beautiful in all the world. When she came, and found that it was Snowdrop alive again, she stood petrified with terror and despair. Then two iron shoes, heated burning hot, were drawn out of the fire with a pair of tongs, and laid before her feet. She was forced to put them on, and to go and dance at Snowdrop's wedding—dancing, dancing on these red hot shoes till she fell down dead.

9

NOT A PIN TO CHOOSE

Once upon a time, in a country in the far East, a merchant was travelling towards the city with three horses loaded with rich goods, and a purse containing a hundred pieces of gold money. The day was very hot, and the road dusty and dry, so that, by and by, when he reached a spot where a cool, clear spring of water came bubbling out from under a rock beneath the shade of a wide-spreading wayside tree, he was glad enough to stop and refresh himself with a draught of the clear coolness and rest awhile. But while he stooped to drink at the fountain, the purse of gold fell from his girdle into the tall grass, and he, not seeing it, let it lie there, and went his way.

Now it chanced that two fagot-makers—the elder by name Ali, the younger Abdallah—who had been in the woods all day chopping fagots, came also travelling the same way, and stopped at the same fountain to drink. There the younger of the two spied the purse lying in the grass, and picked it up. But when he opened it and found it full of gold money, he was like one bereft of wits; he flung his arms, he danced, he shouted, he laughed, he acted like a madman; for never had he seen so much wealth in all of his life before—a hundred pieces of gold money!

Now the older of the two was by nature a merry wag, and though he had never had the chance to taste of pleasure, he thought that nothing in the world could be better worth spending money for than wine and music and dancing. So, when the evening had come, he proposed that they two should go and squander it all at the inn. But the younger fellow—Abdallah— was by nature just as thrifty as the other was spendthrift, and would not consent to waste what he had found. Nevertheless, he was generous and open-hearted, and grudged his friend nothing; so, though he did not care for a wild life himself, he gave Ali a piece of gold to spend as he chose.

By morning every copper of what had been given to the elder fagot-maker was gone, and he had never had such a good time in his life before. All that day and for a week the head of Ali was so full of the memory of the merry night that he had enjoyed that he could think of nothing else. At last, one evening, he asked Abdallah for another piece of gold, and Abdallah gave it to him, and by the next morning it had vanished in the same way that the other had flown. By and by Ali borrowed a third piece of money, and then a fourth and then a fifth, so that by the time that six months had passed and gone he had spent thirty of the hundred pieces that had been found, and in all that time Abdallah had used not so much as a pistareen.

But when Ali came for the thirty-and-first loan, Abdallah refused to let him have any more money. It was in vain that the elder begged and implored—the younger abided by what he had said.

Then Ali began to put on a threatening front. 'You will not let me have the money?' he said.

'No, I will not.'

'You will not?'

'No!'

'Then you shall!' cried Ali; and, so saying, caught the younger fagot-maker by the throat, and began shaking him and shouting, 'Help! Help! I am robbed! I am robbed!' He made such an uproar that half a hundred men, women, and children were gathered around them in less than a minute. 'Here is ingratitude for you!' cried Ali. 'Here is wickedness and thievery! Look at this wretch, all good men, and then turn away your eyes! For twelve years have I lived with this young man as a father might live with a son, and now how does he repay me? He has stolen all that I have in the world—a purse of seventy sequins of gold.'

All this while poor Abdallah had been so amazed that he could do nothing but stand and stare like one stricken dumb; whereupon all the people, thinking him guilty, dragged him off to the judge, reviling him and heaping words of abuse upon him.

Now the judge of that town was known far and near as the 'Wise Judge'; but never had he had such a knotty question as this brought up before him, for by this time Abdallah had found his speech, and swore with a great outcry that the money belonged to him.

But at last a gleam of light came to the Wise Judge in his perplexity. 'Can any one tell me,' said he, 'which of these fellows has had money of late, and which has had none?'

His question was one easily enough answered; a score of people were there to testify that the elder of the two had been living well and spending money freely for six months and more, and a score were also there to swear that Abdallah had lived all the while in penury. 'Then that decides the matter,' said the Wise Judge. 'The money belongs to the elder fagot-maker.'

'But listen, oh my lord judge!' cried Abdallah. 'All that this man has spent I have given to him—I, who found the money. Yes, my lord, I have given it to him, and myself have spent not so much as single mite.'

All who were present shouted with laughter at Abdallah's speech, for who would believe that anyone would be so generous as to spend all upon another and none upon himself?

So poor Abdallah was beaten with rods until he confessed where he had hidden his money; then the Wise Judge handed fifty sequins to Ali and kept twenty himself for his decision, and all went their way praising his justice and judgment.

That is to say, all but poor Abdallah; he went to his home weeping and wailing, and with everyone pointing the finger of scorn at him. He was just as poor as ever, and his back was sore with the beating that he had suffered. All that night he continued to weep and wail, and when the morning had come he was weeping and wailing still.

Now it chanced that a wise man passed that way, and hearing his lamentation, stopped to inquire the cause of his trouble. Abdallah told the other of his sorrow, and the wise man listened, smiling, till he was done, and then he laughed outright. 'My son,' said he, 'if every one in your case should shed tears as abundantly as you have done, the world would have been drowned in salt water by this time. As for your friend, think not ill of him; no man loveth another who is always giving.'

'Nay,' said the young fagot-maker, 'I believe not a word of what you say. Had I been in his place I would have been grateful for the benefits, and not have hated the giver.'

But the wise man only laughed louder than ever. 'Maybe you will have the chance to prove what you say some day,' said he, and went his way, still shaking with his merriment.

Though Abdallah had affirmed that he did not believe what the wise man had said, nevertheless the words of the other were a comfort, for it makes one feel easier in trouble to be told that others have been in a like case with one's self.

So, by and by, Abdallah plucked up some spirit, and, saddling his ass and shouldering his axe, started off to the woods for a bundle of fagots.

Misfortunes, they say, never come single, and so it seemed to be with the fagot-maker that day; for that happened that had never happened to him before—he lost his way in the woods. On he went, deeper and deeper into the thickets, driving his ass before him, bewailing himself and rapping his head with his knuckles. But all his sorrowing helped him nothing, and by the time that night fell he found himself deep in the midst of a great forest full of wild beasts, the very thought of which curdled his blood. He had had nothing to eat all day long, and now the only resting place left him was the branches of some tree. So, unsaddling his ass and leaving it to shift for itself, he climbed to and roosted himself in the crotch of a great limb.

In spite of his hunger he presently fell asleep, for trouble breeds weariness as it breeds grief.

About the dawning of the day he was awakened by the sound of voices and the glaring of lights. He craned his neck and looked down, and there he saw a sight that filled him with amazement: three old men riding each upon a milk-white horse and each bearing a lighted torch in his hand, to light the way through the dark forest.

When they had come just below where Abdallah sat, they dismounted and fastened their several horses to as many trees. Then he who rode first of the three, and who wore a red cap and who seemed to be the chief of them, walked solemnly up to a great rock that stood in the hillside, and, breaking a switch from a shrub that grew in a cleft, struck the face of the stone, crying in a loud voice, 'I command thee to open, in the name of the red Aldebaran!'

Instantly, creaking and groaning, the face of the rock opened like a door, gaping blackly. Then, one after another, the three old men entered, and nothing was left but the dull light of their torches, shining on the walls of the passageway.

What happened inside the cavern the fagot-maker could

neither see nor hear, but minute after minute passed while, he sat as in a maze at all that had happened. Then, presently, he heard a deep thundering voice and a voice as of one of the old men in answer. Then there came a sound swelling louder and louder, as though a great crowd of people were gathering together, and with the voices came the noise of the neighing of horses and the trampling of hoofs. Then at last there came pouring from out the rock a great crowd of horses laden with bales and bundles of rich stuffs and chests and caskets of gold and silver and jewels, and each horse was led by a slave clad in a dress of cloth-of-gold, sparkling and glistening with precious gems. When all these had come out from the cavern, other horses followed, upon each of which sat a beautiful damsel, more lovely than the fancy of man could picture. Beside the damsels marched a guard, each man clad in silver armor, and each bearing a drawn sword that flashed in the brightening day more keenly than the lightning. So they all came pouring forth from the cavern until it seemed as though the whole woods below were filled with the wealth and the beauty of King Solomon's day—and then, last of all, came the three old men.

'In the name of the red Aldebaran,' said he who had bidden the rock to open, 'I command thee to become closed.' Again, creaking and groaning, the rock shut as it had opened—like a door—and the three old men, mounting their horses, led the way from the woods, the others following. The noise and confusion of the many voices shouting and calling, the trample and stamp of horses, grew fainter and fainter, until at last all was once more hushed and still, and only the fagot-maker was left behind, still staring like one dumb and bereft of wits.

But so soon as he was quite sure that all were really gone, he clambered down as quickly as might be. He waited for a while to make doubly sure that no one was left behind, and then he walked straight up to the rock, just as he had seen the old man do. He plucked a switch from the bush, just as he had seen the old man pluck one, and struck the stone, just as the old man had struck it. 'I command thee to open,' said he, 'in the name of the red Aldebaran!'

Instantly, as it had done in answer to the old man's command, there came a creaking and a groaning, and the rock slowly opened like a door, and there was the passageway yawning before him. For a moment or two the fagot-maker hesitated to enter; but all was as still as death, and finally he plucked up courage and went within.

By this time the day was brightening and the sun rising, and by the grey light the fagot-maker could see about him pretty clearly. Not a sign was to be seen of horses or of treasure or of people—nothing but a square block of marble, and upon it a black casket, and upon that again a gold ring, in which was set a blood-red stone. Beyond these things there was nothing; the walls were bare, the roof was bare, the floor was bare—all was bare and naked stone.

'Well,' said the wood chopper, 'as the old men have taken everything else, I might as well take these things. The ring is certainly worth something, and maybe I shall be able to sell the casket for a trifle into the bargain.' So he slipped the ring upon his finger, and, taking up the casket, left the place. 'I command thee to be closed,' said he, 'in the name of the red Aldebaran!' And thereupon the door closed, creaking and groaning.

After a little while he found his ass, saddled it and bridled it, and loaded it with the bundle of fagots that he had chopped the day before, and then set off again to try to find his way out of the thick woods. But still his luck was against him, and the farther he wandered the deeper he found himself in the thickets. In the meantime he was like to die of hunger, for he had not a bite to eat for more than a whole day.

'Perhaps,' said he to himself, 'there may be something

in the casket to stay my stomach;' and, so saying, he sat him down, unlocked the casket, and raised the lid.

Such a yell, as the poor wretch uttered, ears never heard before. Over he rolled upon his back and there lay staring with wide eyes, and away scampered the jackass, kicking up his heels and braying so that the leaves of the trees trembled and shook. For no sooner had he lifted the lid than out leaped a great hideous genie, as black as a coal, with one fiery red eye in the middle of his forehead that glared and rolled most horribly, and with his hands and feet set with claws, sharp and hooked like the talons of a hawk. Poor Abdallah the fagot-maker lay upon his back staring at the monster with a face as white as wax.

'What are thy commands?' said the genie in a terrible voice, that rumbled like the sound of thunder.

'I—I do not know,' said Abdallah, trembling and shaking as with an ague. 'I—I have forgotten.'

'Ask what thou wilt,' said the genie, 'for I must ever obey whomsoever hast the ring that thou wearest upon thy finger. Hath my lord nothing to command wherein I may serve him?'

Abdallah shook his head. 'No,' said he, 'there is nothing—unless—unless you will bring me something to eat.'

'To hear is to obey,' said the genie. 'What will my lord be pleased to have?'

'Just a little bread and cheese,' said Abdallah.

The genie waved his hand, and in an instant a fine damask napkin lay spread upon the ground, and upon it a loaf of bread as white as snow and a piece of cheese such as the king would have been glad to taste. But Abdallah could do nothing but sit staring at the genie, for the sight of the monster quite took away his appetite.

'What more can I do to serve thee?' asked the genie.

'I think,' said Abdallah, 'that I could eat more comfortably if you were away.'

'To hear is to obey,' said the genie. 'Whither shall I go? Shall I enter the casket again?'

'I do not know,' said the fagot-maker; 'how did you come to be there?'

'I am a great genie,' answered the monster, 'and was conjured thither by the great King Solomon, whose seal it is that thou wearest upon thy finger. For a certain fault that I committed I was confined in the box and hidden in the cavern where thou didst find me today. There I lay for thousands of years until one day three old magicians discovered the secret of where I lay hidden. It was they who only this morning compelled me to give them that vast treasure which thou sawest them take away from the cavern not long since.'

'But why did they not take you and the box and the ring away also?' asked Abdallah.

'Because,' answered the genie, 'they are three brothers, and neither two care to trust the other one with such power as the ring has to give, so they made a solemn compact among themselves that I should remain in the cavern, and that no one of the three should visit it without the other two in his company. Now, my lord, if it is thy will that I shall enter the casket again I must even obey thy command in that as in all things; but, if it please thee, I would fain rejoin my own kind again—they from whom I have been parted for so long. Shouldst thou permit me to do so I will still be thy slave, for thou hast only to press the red stone in the ring and repeat these words: By the red Aldebaran, I command thee to come,' and I will be with thee instantly. But if I have my freedom I shall serve thee from gratitude and love, and not from compulsion and with fear.'

'So be it!' said Abdallah. 'I have no choice in the matter, and thou mayest go whither it pleases thee.'

No sooner had the words left his lips than the genie gave a great cry of rejoicing, so piercing that it made Abdallah's flesh creep, and then, fetching the black casket a kick that sent it flying over the tree tops, vanished instantly.

'Well,' quote Abdallah, when he had caught his breath from his amazement, 'these are the most wonderful things that have happened to me in all of my life.' And thereupon he fell to at the bread and cheese, and ate as only a hungry man can eat. When he had finished the last crumb he wiped his mouth with the napkin, and, stretching his arms, felt within him that he was like a new man.

Nevertheless, he was still lost in the woods, and now not even with his ass for comradeship.

He had wandered for quite a little while before he bethought himself of the genie. 'What a fool am I,' said he, 'not to have asked him to help me while he was here.' He pressed his finger upon the ring, and cried in a loud voice, 'By the red Aldebaran, I command thee to come!'

Instantly the genie stood before him—big, black, ugly, and grim. 'What are my lord's commands?' said he.

'I command thee,' said Abdallah the fagot-maker, who was not half so frightened at the sight of the monster this time as he had been before, 'I command thee to help me out of this woods.'

Hardly were the words out of his mouth when the genie snatched Abdallah up, and, flying swifter than the lightning, set him down in the middle of the highway on the outskirts of the forest before he had fairly caught his breath.

When he did gather his wits and looked about him, he knew very well where he was, and that he was upon the road that led to the city. At the sight his heart grew light within him, and off he stepped briskly for home again.

But the sun shone hot and the way was warm and dusty, and before Abdallah had gone very far the sweat was running down his face in streams. After a while he met a rich husbandman riding easily along on an ambling nag, and when Abdallah saw him he rapped his head with his knuckles. 'Why did I not think to ask the genie for a horse?' said he. 'I might just as well have ridden as to have walked, and that upon a horse a hundred times more beautiful than the one that that fellow rides.'

He stepped into the thicket beside the way, where he might be out of sight, and there pressed the stone in his ring, and at his bidding the genie stood before him.

'What are my lord's commands?' said he.

'I would like to have a noble horse to ride upon,' said Abdallah, 'a horse such as a king might use.'

'To hear is to obey,' said the genie; and, stretching out his hand, there stood before Abdallah a magnificent Arab horse, with a saddle and bridle studded with precious stones, and with housings of gold. 'Can I do aught to serve my lord further?' said the genie.

'Not just now,' said Abdallah; 'if I have further use for you I will call you.'

The genie bowed his head and was gone like a flash, and Abdallah mounted his horse and rode off upon his way. But he had not gone far before he drew rein suddenly. 'How foolish must I look,' said he, 'to be thus riding along the high road upon this noble steed, and I myself clad in fagot-maker's rags.' Thereupon he turned his horse into the thicket, and again summoned the genie. 'I should like,' said he, 'to have a suit of clothes fit for a king to wear.'

'My lord shall have that which he desires,' said the genie. He stretched out his hand, and in an instant there lay across his arm raiment such as the eyes of man never saw before—stiff with pearls, and blazing with diamonds and rubies and emeralds and sapphires. The genie himself aided Abdallah to dress, and when he looked down he felt, for the time, quite satisfied.

He rode a little farther. Then suddenly he bethought himself, 'What a silly spectacle shall I cut in the town with no money in my purse and with such fine clothes upon my back.' Once more the genie was summoned. 'I should like,' said the fagot-maker, 'to have a box full of money.'

The genie stretched out his hand, and in it was a casket of mother-of-pearl inlaid with gold and full of money. 'Has my lord any further commands for his servant?' asked he.

'No,' answered Abdallah. 'Stop—I have, too,' he added. 'Yes; I would like to have a young man to carry my money for me.'

'He is here,' said the genie. And there stood a beautiful youth clad in clothes of silver tissue, and holding a milk-white horse by the bridle.

'Stay, genie,' said Abdallah. 'Whilst thou art here thou mayest as well give me enough at once to last me a long time to come. Let me have eleven more caskets of money like this one, and eleven more slaves to carry the same.'

'They are here,' said the genie; and as he spoke there stood eleven more youths before Abdallah, as like the first as so many pictures of the same person, and each youth bore in his hands a box like the one that the monster had given Abdallah. 'Will my lord have anything further?' asked the genie.

'Let me think,' said Abdallah. 'Yes; I know the town well, and that should one so rich as I ride into it without guards he would be certain to be robbed before he had travelled a hundred paces. Let me have an escort of a hundred armed men.'

'It shall be done,' said the genie, and, waving his hand, the road where they stood was instantly filled with armed men, with swords and helmets gleaming and flashing in the sun, and all seated upon magnificently caparisoned horses. 'Can I serve my lord further?' asked the genie.

'No,' said Abdallah the fagot-maker, in admiration, 'I have nothing more to wish for in this world. Thou mayest go, genie, and it will be long ere I will have to call thee again,' and thereupon the genie was gone like a flash.

The captain of Abdallah's troop—a bearded warrior clad in a superb suit of armor—rode up to the fagot-maker, and, leaping from his horse and bowing before him so that his forehead touched the dust, said, 'Whither shall we ride, my lord?'

Abdallah smote his forehead with vexation. 'If I live a thousand years,' said he, 'I will never learn wisdom.' Thereupon, dismounting again, he pressed the ring and summoned the genie. 'I was mistaken,' said he, 'as to not wanting thee so soon. I would have thee build me in the city a magnificent palace, such as man never looked upon before, and let it be full from top to bottom with rich stuffs and treasures of all sorts. And let it have gardens and fountains and terraces fitting for such a place, and let it be meetly served with slaves, both men and women, the most beautiful that are to be found in all the world.'

'Is there aught else that thou wouldst have?' asked the genie.

The fagot-maker meditated a long time. 'I can bethink myself of nothing more just now,' said he.

The genie turned to the captain of the troop and said some words to him in a strange tongue, and then in a moment was gone. The captain gave the order to march, and away they all rode with Abdallah in the midst. 'Who would have thought,' said he, looking around him, with the heart within him swelling with pride as though it would burst—'who would have thought that only this morning I was a poor fagot-maker, lost in the woods and half starved to death? Surely there is nothing left for me to wish for in this world!'

Abdallah was talking of something he knew nothing of.

Never before was such a sight seen in that country, as Abdallah and his troop rode through the gates and into the streets of the city. But dazzling and beautiful as were those who rode attendant upon him, Abdallah the fagot-maker surpassed them all as the moon dims the lustre of the stars. The people crowded around shouting with wonder, and Abdallah, in the fullness of his delight, gave orders to the slaves who bore the caskets of money to open them and to throw the gold to the people. So, with those in the streets scrambling and fighting for the money and shouting and cheering, and others gazing down at the spectacle from the windows and housetops, the fagot-maker and his troop rode slowly along through the town.

Now it chanced that their way led along past the royal palace, and the princess, hearing all the shouting and the hubbub, looked over the edge of the balcony and down into the street. At the same moment Abdallah chanced to look up, and their eyes met. Thereupon the fagot-maker's heart crumbled away within him, for she was the most beautiful princess in all the world. Her eyes were as black as night, her hair like threads of fine silk, her neck like alabaster, and her lips and her cheeks as soft and as red as rose leaves. When she saw that Abdallah was looking at her she dropped the curtain of the balcony and was gone, and the fagot-maker rode away, sighing like a furnace.

So, by and by, he came to his palace, which was built all of marble as white as snow, and which was surrounded with gardens, shaded by flowering trees, and cooled by the plashing of fountains. From the gateway to the door of the palace a carpet of cloth-of-gold had been spread for him to walk upon, and crowds of slaves stood waiting to receive him. But for all these glories Abdallah cared nothing; he hardly looked about him, but, going straight to his room, pressed his ring and summoned the genie.

'What is it that my lord would have?' asked the monster.

'Oh, genie!' said poor Abdallah, 'I would have the princess

for my wife, for without her I am like to die.'

'My lord's commands,' said the genie, 'shall be executed if I have to tear down the city to do so. But perhaps this behest is not so hard to fulfil. First of all, my lord will have to have an ambassador to send to the king.'

'Very well,' said Abdallah with a sigh; 'let me have an ambassador or whatever may be necessary. Only make haste, genie, in thy doings.'

'I shall lose no time,' said the genie; and in a moment was gone.

The king was sitting in council with all of the greatest lords of the land gathered about him, for the Emperor of India had declared war against him, and he and they were in debate, discussing how the country was to be saved. Just then Abdallah's ambassador arrived, and when he and his train entered the council-chamber, all stood up to receive him, for the least of those attendant upon him was more magnificently attired than the king himself, and was bedecked with such jewels as the royal treasury could not match.

Kneeling before the king, the ambassador touched the ground with his forehead. Then, still kneeling, he unrolled a scroll, written in letters of gold, and from it read the message asking for the princess as wife for the Lord Abdallah.

When he had ended, the king sat for a while stroking his beard and meditating. But before he spoke the oldest lord of the council arose and said: 'O sire! If this Lord Abdallah who asks for the princess for his wife can send such a magnificent company in the train of his ambassador, may it not be that he may be able also to help you in your war against the Emperor of India?'

'True!' said the king. Then turning to the ambassador: 'Tell your master,' said he, 'that if he will furnish me with an army of one hundred thousand men, to aid me in the war against the Emperor of India, he shall have my daughter for his wife.'

'Sire,' said the ambassador, 'I will answer now for my master, and the answer shall be this: That he will help you with an army, not of one hundred thousand, but of two hundred thousand men. And if tomorrow you will be pleased to ride forth to the plain that lieth to the south of the city, my Lord Abdallah will meet you there with his army.' Then, once more bowing, he withdrew from the council-chamber, leaving all of them that were there amazed at what had happened.

So the next day the king and all his court rode out to the place appointed. As they drew near they saw that the whole face of the plain was covered with a mighty host, drawn up in troops and squadrons. As the king rode towards this vast army, Abdallah met him, surrounded by his generals. He dismounted and would have kneeled, but the king would not permit him, but, raising him, kissed him upon the cheek, calling him son. Then the king and Abdallah rode down before the ranks and the whole army waved their swords, and the flashing of the sunlight on the blades was like lightning, and they shouted, and the noise was like the pealing of thunder.

Before Abdallah marched off to the wars he and the princess were married, and for a whole fortnight nothing was heard but the sound of rejoicing. The city was illuminated from end to end, and all of the fountains ran with wine instead of water. And of all those who rejoiced, none was so happy as the princess, for never had she seen one whom she thought so grand and noble and handsome as her husband. After the fortnight had passed and gone, the army marched away to the wars with Abdallah at its head.

Victory after victory followed, for in every engagement the Emperor of India's troops were driven from the field. In two months' time the war was over and Abdallah marched back again—the greatest general in the world. But it was no longer as Abdallah that he was known, but as the Emperor of India, for the former emperor had been killed in the war, and Abdallah had set the crown upon his own head.

The little taste that he had had of conquest had given him an appetite for more, so that with the armies the genie provided him he conquered all the neighboring countries and brought them under his rule. So he became the greatest emperor in all the world; kings and princes kneeled before him, and he, Abdallah, the fagot-maker, looking about him, could say: 'No one in all the world is so great as I!'

Could he desire anything more?

Yes; he did! He desired to be rid of the genie!

When he thought of how all that he was in power and might—he, the Emperor of the World—how all his riches and all his glory had come as gifts from a hideous black monster with only one eye, his heart was filled with bitterness. 'I cannot forget,' said he to himself, 'that as he has given me all these things, he may take them all away again. Suppose that I should lose my ring and that some one else should find it; who knows but that they might become as great as I, and strip me of everything, as I have stripped others. Yes; I wish he was out of the way!'

Once, when such thoughts as these were passing through his mind, he was paying a visit to his father-in-law, the king. He was walking up and down the terrace of the garden meditating on these matters, when, leaning over a wall and looking down into the street, he saw a fagot-maker—just such a fagot-maker as he himself had one time been—driving an ass—just such an ass as he had one time driven. The fagot-maker carried something under his arm, and what should it be but the very casket in which the genie had once been imprisoned, and which he—the one-time fagot-maker—had seen the genie kick over the tree-tops.

The sight of the casket put a sudden thought into his mind. He shouted to his attendants, and bade them haste and bring the fagot-maker to him. Off they ran, and in a little while came dragging the poor wretch, trembling and as white as death; for he thought nothing less than that his end had certainly come. As soon as those who had seized him had loosened their hold, he flung himself prostrate at the feet of the Emperor Abdallah, and there lay like one dead.

'Where didst thou get yonder casket?' asked the emperor.

'Oh, my lord!' croaked the poor fagot-maker, 'I found it out yonder in the woods.'

'Give it to me,' said the emperor, 'and my treasurer shall count thee out a thousand pieces of gold in exchange.'

So soon as he had the casket safe in his hands he hurried away to his privy chamber, and there pressed the red stone in his ring. 'In the name of the red Aldebaran, I command thee to appear!' said he, and in a moment the genie stood before him.

'What are my lord's commands?' said he.

'I would have thee enter this casket again,' said the Emperor Abdallah.

'Enter the casket!' cried the genie, aghast.

'Enter the casket.'

'In what have I done anything to offend my lord?' said the genie.

'In nothing,' said the emperor; 'only I would have thee enter the casket again as thou wert when I first found thee.'

It was in vain that the genie begged and implored for mercy, it was in vain that he reminded Abdallah of all that he had done to benefit him; the great emperor stood as hard as a rock—into the casket the genie must and should go. So at last into the casket the monster went, bellowing most lamentably.

The Emperor Abdallah shut the lid of the casket, and locked it and sealed it with his seal. Then, hiding it under his cloak, he bore it out into the garden and to a deep well, and, first making sure that nobody was by to see, dropped casket and genie and all into the water.

Now had that wise man been by—the wise man who had laughed so when the poor young fagot-maker wept and wailed at the ingratitude of his friend—the wise man who had laughed still louder when the young fagot-maker vowed that in another case he would not have been so ungrateful to one who had benefited him—how that wise man would have roared when he heard the casket plump into the waters of the well! For, upon my word of honor, betwixt Ali the fagot-maker and Abdallah the Emperor of the World there was not a pin to choose, except in degree.

10

A PIECE OF GOOD LUCK

There were three students who were learning all that they could. The first was named Joseph, the second was named John, and the third was named Jacob Stuck. They studied seven long years under a wise master, and in that time they learned all that their master had to teach them of the wonderful things he knew. They learned all about geometry, they learned all about algebra, they learned all about astronomy, they learned all about the hidden arts, they learned all about everything, except how to mend their own hose and where to get cabbage to boil in the pot.

And now they were to go out into the world to practise what they knew. The master called the three students to him—the one named Joseph, the second named John, and the third named Jacob Stuck—and said he to them: 'You have studied faithfully and have learned all that I have been able to teach you, and now you shall not go out into the world with nothing at all. See; here are three glass balls, and that is one for each of you. Their like is not to be found in the four corners of the world. Carry the balls wherever you go, and when one of them drops to the ground, dig, and there you will certainly find a treasure.'

So the three students went out into the wide world.

Well, they travelled on and on for day after day, each carrying his glass ball with him wherever he went. They travelled on and on for I cannot tell how long, until one day the ball that Joseph carried slipped out of his fingers and fell to the ground. 'I've found a treasure!' cried Joseph, 'I've found a treasure!'

The three students fell to work scratching and digging where the ball had fallen, and by and by they found something. It was a chest with an iron ring in the lid. It took all three of them to haul it up out of the ground, and when they did so they found it was full to the brim of silver money.

Were they happy? Well, they were happy! They danced around and around the chest, for they had never seen so much money in all their lives before. 'Brothers,' said Joseph, in exultation, 'here is enough for all hands, and it shall be share and share alike with us, for haven't we studied seven long years together?' And so for a while they were as happy as happy could be.

But by and by a flock of second thoughts began to buzz in the heads of John and Jacob Stuck. 'Why,' said they, 'as for that, to be sure, a chest of silver money is a great thing for three students to find who had nothing better than book learning to help them along; but who knows but that there is something better even than silver money out in the wide world?' So, after all, and in spite of the chest of silver money they had found, the two of them were for going on to try their fortunes a little farther. And as for Joseph, why, after all, when he came to think of it, he was not sorry to have his chest of silver money all to himself.

So the two travelled on and on for a while, here and there and everywhere, until at last it was John's ball that slipped out of his fingers and fell to the ground. They dug where it fell, and this time it was a chest of gold money they found.

Yes, a chest of gold money! A chest of real gold money!

They just stood and stared and stared, for if they had not seen it they would not have believed that such a thing could have been in the world. 'Well, Jacob Stuck,' said John, 'it was well to travel a bit farther than poor Joseph did, was it not? What is a chest of silver money to such a treasure as this? Come, brother, here is enough to make us both rich for all the rest of our lives. We need look for nothing better than this.'

But no; by and by Jacob Stuck began to cool down again, and now that second thoughts were coming to him he would not even be satisfied with a half-share of a chest of gold money. No; maybe there might be something better than even a chest full of gold money to be found in the world. As for John, why, after all, he was just as well satisfied to keep his treasure for himself. So the two shook hands, and then Jacob Stuck jogged away alone, leaving John stuffing his pockets and his hat full of gold money, and I should have liked to have been there, to have had my share.

Well, Jacob Stuck jogged on and on by himself, until after a while he came to a great, wide desert, where there was not a blade or a stick to be seen far or near. He jogged on and on, and he wished he had not come there. He jogged on and on when all of a sudden the glass ball he carried slipped out of his fingers and fell to the ground.

'Aha!' said he to himself, 'now maybe I shall find some great treasure compared to which even silver and gold are as nothing at all.'

He dug down into the barren earth of the desert; and he dug and he dug, but neither silver nor gold did he find. He dug and dug; and by and by, at last, he did find something. And what was it? Why, nothing but something that looked like a piece of blue glass not a big bigger than my thumb. 'Is that all?' said Jacob Stuck. 'And have I travelled all this weary way and into the blinding desert only for this? Have I passed by silver and gold enough to make me rich for all my life, only to find a little piece of blue glass?'

Jacob Stuck did not know what he had found. I shall tell you what it was. It was a solid piece of good luck without flaw or blemish, and it was almost the only piece I ever heard tell of. Yes; that was what it was—a solid piece of good luck; and as for Jacob Stuck, why, he was not the first in the world by many and one over who has failed to know a piece of good luck when they have found it. Yes; it looked just like a piece of blue glass no bigger than my thumb, and nothing else.

'Is that all?' said Jacob Stuck. 'And have I travelled all this weary way and into the blinding desert only for this? Have I passed by silver and gold enough to make me rich for all my life, only to find a little piece of blue glass?'

He looked at the bit of glass, and he turned it over and over in his hand. It was covered with dirt. Jacob Stuck blew his breath upon it, and rubbed it with his thumb.

Crack! Dong! Bang! Smash!

Upon my word, had a bolt of lightning burst at Jacob Stuck's feet he could not have been more struck of a heap. For no sooner had he rubbed the glass with his thumb than with a noise like a clap of thunder there instantly stood before him a great, big man, dressed in clothes as red as a flame, and with eyes that shone sparks of fire. It was the Genie of Good Luck. It nearly knocked Jacob Stuck off his feet to see him there so suddenly.

'What will you have?' said the genie. 'I am the slave of good luck. Whosoever holds that piece of crystal in his hand ,him must I obey in whatsoever he may command.'

'Do you mean that you are my servant and that I am your master?' said Jacob Stuck.

'Yes; command and I obey.'

'Why, then,' said Jacob Stuck, 'I would like you to help me

out of this desert place, if you can do so, for it is a poor spot for any Christian soul to be.'

'To hear is to obey,' said the genie, and, before Jacob Stuck knew what had happened to him, the genie had seized him and was flying with him through the air swifter than the wind. On and on he flew, and the earth seemed to slide away beneath. On and on flew the flame-colored genie until at last he set Jacob down in a great meadow where there was a river. Beyond the river were the white walls and grand houses of the king's town.

'Hast thou any further commands?' said the genie.

'Tell me what you can do for me?' said Jacob Stuck.

'I can do whatsoever thou mayest order me to do,' said the genie.

'Well, then,' said Jacob Stuck, 'I think first of all I would like to have plenty of money to spend.'

'To hear is to obey,' said the genie, and, as he spoke, he reached up into the air and picked out a purse from nothing at all. 'Here,' said he, 'is the purse of fortune; take from it all that thou needest and yet it will always be full. As long as thou hast it thou shalt never be lacking riches.'

'I am very much obliged to you,' said Jacob Stuck. 'I've learned geometry and algebra and astronomy and the hidden arts, but I never heard tell of anything like this before.'

So Jacob Stuck went into the town with all the money he could spend, and such a one is welcome anywhere. He lacked nothing that money could buy. He bought himself a fine house; he made all the friends he wanted, and more; he lived without a care, and with nothing to do but to enjoy himself. That was what a bit of good luck did for him.

Now the princess, the daughter of the king of that town, was the most beautiful in all the world, but so proud and haughty that her like was not to be found within the bounds of all the seven rivers. So proud was she and so haughty that she would neither look upon a young man nor allow any young man to look upon her. She was so particular that whenever she went out to take a ride a herald was sent through the town with a trumpet ordering that every house should be closed and that everybody should stay within doors, so that the princess should run no risk of seeing a young man, or that no young man by chance should see her.

One day the herald went through the town blowing his trumpet and calling in a great, loud voice: 'Close your doors! Close your windows! Her highness, the princess, comes to ride; let no man look upon her on pain of death!'

Thereupon everybody began closing their doors and windows, and, as it was with the others, so it was with Jacob Stuck's house; it had, like all the rest, to be shut up as tight as a jug.

But Jacob Stuck was not satisfied with that; not he. He was for seeing the princess, and he was bound he would do so. So he bored a hole through the door, and when the princess came riding by he peeped out at her.

Jacob Stuck thought he had never seen anyone so beautiful in all his life. It was like the sunlight shining in his eyes, and he almost sneezed. Her cheeks were like milk and rose leaves, and her hair like fine threads of gold. She sat in a golden coach with a golden crown upon her head, and Jacob Stuck stood looking and looking until his heart melted within him like wax in the oven. Then the princess was gone, and Jacob Stuck stood there sighing and sighing.

'Oh, dear! Dear!' said he, 'what shall I do? For, proud as she is, I must see her again or else I will die of it.'

All that day he sat sighing and thinking about the beautiful princess, until the evening had come. Then he suddenly thought of his piece of good luck. He pulled his piece of blue glass out of his pocket and breathed upon it and rubbed it with his thumb, and instantly the genie was there.

This time Jacob Stuck was not frightened at all.

'What are thy commands, O master?' said the genie.

'O genie!' said Jacob Stuck, 'I have seen the princess today, and it seems to me that there is nobody like her in all the world. Tell me, could you bring her here so that I might see her again?'

'Yes,' said the genie, 'I could.'

'Then do so,' said Jacob Stuck, 'and I will have you prepare a grand feast, and have musicians to play beautiful music, for I would have the princess sup with me.'

'To hear is to obey,' said the genie. As he spoke he smote his hands together, and instantly there appeared twenty musicians, dressed in cloth of gold and silver. With them they brought hautboys and fiddles, big and little, and flageolets and drums and horns, and this and that to make music with. Again the genie smote his hands together, and instantly there appeared fifty servants dressed in silks and satins and spangled with jewels, who began to spread a table with fine linen embroidered with gold, and to set plates of gold and silver upon it. The genie smote his hands together a third time, and in answer there came six servants. They led Jacob Stuck into another room, where there was a bath of musk and rose water. They bathed him in the bath and dressed him in clothes like an emperor, and when he came out again his face shone, and he was as handsome as a picture.

Then by and by he knew that the princess was coming, for suddenly there was the sound of girls' voices singing and the twanging of stringed instruments. The door flew open, and in came a crowd of beautiful girls, singing and playing music, and after them the princess herself, more beautiful than ever. But the proud princess was frightened! Yes, she was. And well she might be, for the genie had flown with her through the air from the palace, and that is enough to frighten anybody. Jacob

Stuck came to her all glittering and shining with jewels and gold, and took her by the hand. He led her up the hall, and as he did so the musicians struck up and began playing the most beautiful music in the world. Then Jacob Stuck and the princess sat down to supper and began eating and drinking, and Jacob Stuck talked of all the sweetest things he could think of. Thousands of wax candles made the palace bright as day, and as the princess looked about her she thought she had never seen anything so fine in all the world. After they had eaten their supper and ended with a dessert of all kinds of fruits and of sweetmeats, the door opened and there came a beautiful young servinglad, carrying a silver tray, upon which was something wrapped in a napkin. He kneeled before Jacob Stuck and held the tray, and from the napkin Jacob Stuck took a necklace of diamonds, each stone as big as a pigeon's egg.

'This is to remind you of me,' said Jacob Stuck, 'when you have gone home again.' And as he spoke he hung it around the princess's neck.

Just then the clock struck twelve.

Hardly had the last stroke sounded when every light was snuffed out, and all was instantly dark and still. Then, before she had time to think, the Genie of Good Luck snatched the princess up once more and flew back to the palace more swiftly than the wind. And, before the princess knew what had happened to her, there she was.

It was all so strange that the princess might have thought it was a dream, only for the necklace of diamonds, the like of which was not to be found in all the world.

The next morning there was a great buzzing in the palace, you may be sure. The princess told all about how she had been carried away during the night, and had supped in such a splendid palace, and with such a handsome man dressed like an emperor. She showed her necklace of diamonds, and the king and his prime minister could not look at it or wonder at it enough. The prime minister and the king talked and talked the matter over together, and every now and then the proud princess put in a word of her own.

'Anybody,' said the prime minister, 'can see with half an eye that it is all magic, or else it is a wonderful piece of good luck. Now, I'll tell you what shall be done,' said he. 'The princess shall keep a piece of chalk by her; and, if she is carried away again in such a fashion, she shall mark a cross with the piece of chalk on the door of the house to which she is taken. Then we shall find the rogue that is playing such a trick, and that quickly enough.'

'Yes,' said the king; 'that is very good advice.'

'I will do it,' said the princess.

All that day Jacob Stuck sat thinking and thinking about the beautiful princess. He could not eat a bite, and he could hardly wait for the night to come. As soon as it had fallen, he breathed upon his piece of glass and rubbed his thumb upon it, and there stood the genie of Good Luck.

'I'd like the princess here again,' said he, 'as she was last night, with feasting and drinking, such as we had before.'

'To hear is to obey,' said the genie.

And as it had been the night before, so it was now. The genie brought the princess, and she and Jacob Stuck feasted together until nearly midnight. Then, again, the door opened, and the beautiful servantlad came with the tray and something upon it covered with a napkin. Jacob Stuck unfolded the napkin, and this time it was a cup made of a single ruby, and filled to the brim with gold money. And the wonder of the cup was this: that no matter how much money you took out of it, it was always full. 'Take this,' said Jacob Stuck, 'to remind you of me.' Then the clock struck twelve, and instantly all was darkness, and the genie carried the princess home again.

But the princess had brought her piece of chalk with her, as the prime minister had advised; and in some way or other she contrived, either in coming or going, to mark a cross upon the door of Jacob Stuck's house.

But, clever as she was, the Genie of Good Luck was more clever still. He saw what the princess did; and, as soon as he had carried her home, he went all through the town and marked a cross upon every door, great and small, little and big, just as the princess had done upon the door of Jacob Stuck's house, only upon the prime minister's door he put two crosses. The next morning everybody was wondering what all the crosses on the house-doors meant, and the king and the prime minister were no wiser than they had been before.

But the princess had brought the ruby cup with her, and she and the king could not look at it and wonder at it enough.

'Pooh!' said the prime minister; 'I tell you it is nothing else in the world but just a piece of good luck—that is all it is. As for the rogue who is playing all these tricks, let the princess keep a pair of scissors by her, and, if she is carried away again, let her contrive to cut off a lock of his hair from over the young man's right ear. Then tomorrow we will find out who has been trimmed.'

Yes, the princess would do that; so, before evening was come, she tied a pair of scissors to her belt.

Well, Jacob Stuck could hardly wait for the night to come to summon the Genie of Good Luck. 'I want to sup with the princess again,' said he.

'To hear is to obey,' said the Genie of Good Luck; and, as soon as he had made everything ready, away he flew to fetch the princess again.

Well, they feasted and drank, and the music played, and the candles were as bright as day, and beautiful girls sang and danced, and Jacob Stuck was as happy as a king. But the princess kept her scissors by her, and, when Jacob Stuck was not looking, she contrived to snip off a lock of his hair from over his right ear, and nobody saw what was done but the Genie of Good Luck.

And it came towards midnight.

Once more the door opened, and the beautiful servinglad came into the room, carrying the tray of silver with something upon it wrapped in a napkin. This time Jacob Stuck gave the princess an emerald ring for a keepsake, and the wonder of it was that every morning two other rings just like it would drop from it.

Then twelve o'clock sounded, the lights went out, and the genie took the princess home again.

But the genie had seen what the princess had done. As soon as he had taken her safe home, he struck his palms together and summoned all his companions. 'Go,' said he, 'throughout the town and trim a lock of hair from over the right ear of every man in the whole place;' and so they did, from the king himself to the beggar-man at the gates. As for the prime minister, the genie himself trimmed two locks of hair from him, one from over each of his ears, so that the next morning he looked as shorn as an old sheep. In the morning all the town was in a hubbub, and everybody was wondering how all the men came to have their hair clipped as it was. But the princess had brought the lock of Jacob Stuck's hair away with her wrapped up in a piece of paper, and there it was.

As for the ring Jacob Stuck had given to her, why, the next morning there were three of them, and the king thought he had never heard tell of such a wonderful thing.

'I tell you,' said the prime minister, 'there is nothing in it but a piece of good luck, and not a grain of virtue. It's just a piece of good luck—that's all it is.'

'No matter,' said the king; 'I never saw the like of it in all my life before. And now, what are we going to do?'

The prime minister could think of nothing.

Then the princess spoke up. 'Your majesty,' she said, 'I can find the young man for you. Just let the herald go through the town and proclaim that I will marry the young man to whom this lock of hair belongs, and then we will find him quickly enough.'

'What!' cried the prime minister; 'will, then, the princess marry a man who has nothing better than a little bit of good luck to help him along in the world?'

'Yes,' said the princess, 'I shall if I can find him.'

So the herald was sent out around the town proclaiming that the princess would marry the man to whose head belonged the lock of hair that she had.

A lock of hair! Why, every man had lost a lock of hair! Maybe the princess could fit it on again, and then the fortune of him to whom it belonged would be made. All the men in the town crowded up to the king's palace. But all for no use, for never a one of them was fitted with his own hair.

As for Jacob Stuck, he too had heard what the herald had proclaimed. Yes; he too had heard it, and his heart jumped and hopped within him like a young lamb in the springtime. He knew whose hair it was the princess had. Away he went by himself, and rubbed up his piece of blue glass, and there stood the genie.

'What are thy commands?' said he.

'I am,' said Jacob Stuck, 'going up to the king's palace to marry the princess, and I would have a proper escort.'

'To hear is to obey,' said the genie.

He smote his hands together, and instantly there appeared a score of attendants who took Jacob Stuck, and led him into another room, and began clothing him in a suit so magnificent that it dazzled the eyes to look at it. He smote his hands together again, and out in the courtyard there appeared a troop of horsemen to escort Jacob Stuck to the palace, and they were all clad in gold and silver armour. He smote his hands together again, and there appeared twenty-and-one horses—twenty as black as night and one as white as milk, and it twinkled and sparkled all over with gold and jewels, and at the head of each horse of the one-and-twenty horses stood a slave clad in crimson velvet to hold the bridle. Again he smote his hands together, and there appeared in the anteroom twenty handsome young men, each with a marble bowl filled with gold money, and when Jacob Stuck came out dressed in his fine clothes, there they all were.

Jacob Stuck mounted upon the horse as white as milk, the young men mounted each upon one of the black horses, the troopers in the gold and silver armour wheeled their horses, the trumpets blew, and away they rode—such a sight as was never seen in that town before, when they had come out into the streets. The young men with the basins scattered the gold money to the people, and a great crowd ran scrambling after, and shouted and cheered.

So Jacob Stuck rode up to the king's palace, and the king himself came out to meet him with the princess hanging on his arm.

As for the princess, she knew him the moment she laid eyes on him. She came down the steps, and set the lock of hair against his head, where she had trimmed it off the night before, and it fitted and matched exactly. 'This is the young man,' said she, 'and I will marry him, and none other.'

But the prime minister whispered and whispered in the king's ear: 'I tell you this young man is nobody at all,' said he, 'but just some fellow who has had a little bit of good luck.'

'Pooh!' said the king, 'stuff and nonsense! Just look at all the gold and jewels and horses and men. What will you do,' said he to Jacob Stuck, 'if I let you marry the princess?'

'I will,' said Jacob Stuck, 'build for her the finest palace that ever was seen in all this world.'

'Very well,' said the king, 'yonder are those sand hills over there. You shall remove them and build your palace there. When it is finished you shall marry the princess.' For if he does that, thought the king to himself, it is something better than mere good luck.

'It shall,' said Jacob Stuck, 'be done by tomorrow morning.'

Well, all that day Jacob Stuck feasted and made merry at the king's palace, and the king wondered when he was going to begin to build his palace. But Jacob Stuck said nothing at all; he just feasted and drank and made merry. When night had come, however, it was all different. Away he went by himself, and blew his breath upon his piece of blue glass, and rubbed it with his thumb. Instantly there stood the genie before him. 'What wouldst thou have?' said he.

'I would like,' said Jacob Stuck, 'to have the sand hills over yonder carried away, and a palace built there of white marble and gold and silver, such as the world never saw before. And let there be gardens planted there with flowering plants and trees, and let there be fountains and marble walks. And let there be servants and attendants in the palace of all sorts and kinds—men and women. And let there be a splendid feast spread for tomorrow morning, for then I am going to marry the princess.'

'To hear is to obey,' said the genie, and instantly he was gone.

All night there was from the sand hills a ceaseless sound as of thunder—a sound of banging and clapping and hammering and sawing and calling and shouting. All that night the sounds continued unceasingly, but at daybreak all was still, and when the sun arose there stood the most splendid palace it ever looked down upon; shining as white as snow, and blazing with gold and silver. All around it were gardens and fountains and orchards. A great highway had been built between it and the king's palace, and all along the highway a carpet of cloth of gold had been spread for the princess to walk upon.

Dear! Dear! How all the town stared with wonder when they saw such a splendid palace standing where the day before had been nothing but naked sand hills! The folk flocked in crowds to see it, and all the country about was alive with people coming and going. As for the king, he could not believe his eyes when he saw it. He stood with the princess and looked and looked. Then came Jacob Stuck. 'And now,' said he, 'am I to marry the princess?'

'Yes,' cried the king in admiration, 'you are!'

So Jacob Stuck married the princess, and a splendid wedding it was. That was what a little bit of good luck did for him.

After the wedding was over, it was time to go home to the grand new palace. Then there came a great troop of horsemen with shining armor and with music, sent by the genie to escort Jacob Stuck and the princess and the king and the prime minister to Jacob Stuck's new palace. They rode along over the carpet of gold, and such a fine sight was never seen in that land before. As they drew near to the palace a great crowd of servants, clad in silks and satins and jewels, came out to meet them, singing and dancing and playing on harps and lutes. The king and the princess thought that they must be dreaming.

'All this is yours,' said Jacob Stuck to the princess; and he was that fond of her, he would have given her still more if he could have thought of anything else.

Jacob Stuck and the princess, and the king and the prime minister, all went into the palace, and there was a splendid feast spread in plates of pure gold and silver, and they, all four, sat down together.

But the prime minister was as sour about it all as a crabapple. All the time they were feasting he kept whispering and whispering in the king's ear. 'It is all stuff and nonsense,' said he, 'for such a man as Jacob Stuck to do all this by himself. I tell you, it is all a piece of good luck, and not a bit of merit in it.'

He whispered and whispered, until at last the king up and spoke. 'Tell me, Jacob Stuck,' he said, 'where do you get all these fine things?'

'It all comes of a piece of good luck,' said Jacob Stuck.

'That is what I told you,' said the prime minister.

'A piece of good luck!' said the king. 'Where did you come across such a piece of good luck?'

'I found it,' said Jacob Stuck.

'Found it!' said the king; 'and have you got it with you now?'

'Yes, I have,' said Jacob Stuck; 'I always carry it about with me;' and he thrust his hand into his pocket and brought out his piece of blue crystal.

'That!' said the king. 'Why, that is nothing but a piece of blue glass!'

'That,' said Jacob Stuck, 'is just what I thought till I found out better. It is no common piece of glass, I can tell you. You just breathe upon it so, and rub your thumb upon it thus, and instantly a genie dressed in red comes to do all that he is bidden. That is how it is.'

'I should like to see it,' said the king.

'So you shall,' said Jacob Stuck; 'here it is,' said he; and he reached it across the table to the prime minister to give it to the king.

Yes, that was what he did; he gave it to the prime minister to give it to the king. The prime minister had been listening to all that had been said, and he knew what he was about. He took what Jacob Stuck gave him, and he had never had such a piece of luck come to him before.

And did the prime minister give it to the king, as Jacob Stuck had intended? Not a bit of it. No sooner had he got it safe in his hand, than he blew his breath upon it and rubbed it with his thumb.

Crack! Dong! Boom! Crash!

There stood the genie, like a flash and as red as fire. The princess screamed out and nearly fainted at the sight, and the poor king sat trembling like a rabbit.

'Whosoever possesses that piece of blue crystal,' said the genie, in a terrible voice, 'him must I obey. What are thy commands?'

'Take this king,' cried the prime minister, 'and take Jacob Stuck, and carry them both away into the farthest part of the desert whence the fellow came.'

'To hear is to obey,' said the genie; and instantly he seized the king in one hand and Jacob Stuck in the other, and flew away with them swifter than the wind. On and on he flew, and the earth seemed to slide away beneath them like a cloud. On and on he flew until he had come to the farthest part of the desert. There he sat them both down, and it was as pretty a pickle as ever the king or Jacob Stuck had been in, in all of their lives. Then the genie flew back again whence he had come.

There sat the poor princess crying and crying, and there sat the prime minister trying to comfort her. 'Why do you cry?' said he; 'why are you afraid of me? I will do you no harm. Listen,' said he; 'I will use this piece of good luck in a way that Jacob Stuck would never have thought of. I will make myself king. I will conquer the world, and make myself emperor over all the earth. Then I will make you my queen.'

But the poor princess cried and cried.

'Hast thou any further commands?' said the genie.

'Not now,' said the prime minister; 'you may go now;' and the genie vanished like a puff of smoke.

But the princess cried and cried.

The prime minister sat down beside her. 'Why do you cry?' said he.

'Because I am afraid of you,' said she.

'And why are you afraid of me?' said he.

'Because of that piece of blue glass. You will rub it again, and then that great red monster will come again to frighten me.'

'I will rub it no more,' said he.

'Oh, but you will,' said she; 'I know you will.'

'I will not,' said he.

'But I can't trust you,' said she 'as long as you hold it in your hand.'

'Then I will lay it aside,' said he, and so he did. Yes, he did; and he is not the first man who has thrown aside a piece of good luck for the sake of a pretty face. 'Now are you afraid of me?' said he.

'No, I am not,' said she; and she reached out her hand as though to give it to him. But, instead of doing so, she snatched up the piece of blue glass as quick as a flash.

'Now,' said she, 'it is my turn;' and then the prime minister knew that his end had come.

She blew her breath upon the piece of blue glass and rubbed her thumb upon it. Instantly, as with a clap of thunder, the great red genie stood before her, and the poor prime minister sat shaking and trembling.

'Whosoever hath that piece of blue crystal,' said the genie, 'that one must I obey. What are your orders, O princess?'

'Take this man,' cried the princess, 'and carry him away into the desert where you took those other two, and bring my father and Jacob Stuck back again.'

'To hear is to obey,' said the genie, and instantly he seized the prime minister, and, in spite of the poor man's kicks and struggles, snatched him up and flew away with him swifter than the wind. On and on he flew until he had come to the farthest part of the desert, and there sat the king and Jacob Stuck still thinking about things. Down he dropped the prime minister, up he picked the king and Jacob Stuck, and away he flew swifter than the wind. On and on he flew until he had brought the two back to the palace again; and there sat the princess waiting for them, with the piece of blue crystal in her hand.

'You have saved us!' cried the king.

'You have saved us!' cried Jacob Stuck. 'Yes, you have saved us, and you have my piece of good luck into the bargain. Give it to me again.'

'I will do nothing of the sort,' said the princess. 'If the menfolk think no more of a piece of good luck than to hand it round like a bit of broken glass, it is better for the womenfolk to keep it for them.'

And there, to my mind, she brewed good common sense, that needed no skimming to make it fit for Jacob Stuck, or for any other man, for the matter of that.

And now for the end of this story. Jacob Stuck lived with his princess in his fine palace as grand as a king, and when the old king died he became the king after him.

One day there came two men travelling along, and they were footsore and weary. They stopped at Jacob Stuck's palace and asked for something to eat. Jacob Stuck did not know them at first, and then he did. One was Joseph and the other was John.

This is what had happened to them:

Joseph had sat and sat where John and Jacob Stuck had left him on his box of silver money, until a band of thieves had come along and robbed him of it all. John had carried away his pockets and his hat full of gold, and had lived like a prince as long as it had lasted. Then he had gone back for more, but in the meantime some rogue had come along and had stolen it all. Yes, that was what had happened, and now they were as poor as ever.

Jacob Stuck welcomed them and brought them in and made much of them.

Well, the truth is truth, and this is it: It is better to have a little bit of good luck to help one in what one undertakes than to have a chest of silver or a chest of gold.

11

THE SALT OF LIFE

Once upon a time there was a king who had three sons, and by the time that the youngest prince had down upon his chin the king had grown so old that the cares of the kingdom began to rest over-heavily upon his shoulders. So he called his chief councillor and told him that he was of a mind to let the princes reign in his stead. To the son who loved him the best he would give the largest part of his kingdom, to the son who loved him the next best the next part, and to the son who loved him the least the least part. The old councillor was very wise and shook his head, but the king's mind had long been settled as to what he was about to do. So he called the princes to him one by one and asked each as to how much he loved him.

'I love you as a mountain of gold,' said the oldest prince, and the king was very pleased that his son should give him such love.

'I love you as a mountain of silver,' said the second prince, and the king was pleased with that also.

But when the youngest prince was called, he did not answer at first, but thought and thought. At last he looked up. 'I love you,' said he, 'as I love salt.'

When the king heard what his youngest son said he was filled with anger. 'What!' he cried, 'do you love me no better than salt—a stuff that is the most bitter of all things to the taste, and the cheapest and the commonest of all things in the world? Away with you, and never let me see your face again! Henceforth you are no son of mine.'

The prince would have spoken, but the king would not allow him, and bade his guards thrust the young man forth from the room.

Now the queen loved the youngest prince the best of all her sons, and when she heard how the king was about to drive him forth into the wide world to shift for himself, she wept and wept. 'Ah, my son!' said she to him, 'it is little or nothing that I have to give you. Nevertheless, I have one precious thing. Here is a ring; take it and wear it always, for so long as you have it upon your finger no magic can have power over you.'

Thus it was that the youngest prince set forth into the wide world with little or nothing but a ring upon his finger.

For seven days he travelled on, and knew not where he was going or whither his footsteps led. At the end of that time he came to the gates of a town. The prince entered the gates, and found himself in a city the like of which he had never seen in his life before for grandeur and magnificence—beautiful palaces and gardens, stores and bazaars crowded with rich stuffs of satin and silk and wrought silver and gold of cunningest workmanship; for the land to which he had come was the richest in all of the world. All that day he wandered up and down, and thought nothing of weariness and hunger for wonder of all that he saw. But at last evening drew down, and he began to bethink himself of somewhere to lodge during the night.

Just then he came to a bridge, over the wall of which leaned an old man with a long white beard, looking down into the water. He was dressed richly but soberly, and every now and then he sighed and groaned, and as the prince drew near he saw the tears falling—drip, drip—from the old man's eyes.

The prince had a kind heart, and could not bear to see one in distress; so he spoke to the old man, and asked him his trouble.

'Ah, me!' said the other, 'only yesterday I had a son, tall and handsome like yourself. But the queen took him to sup with her, and I am left all alone in my old age, like a tree stripped of leaves and fruit.'

'But surely,' said the prince, 'it can be no such sad matter to sup with a queen. That is an honor that most men covet.'

'Ah!' said the old man, 'you are a stranger in this place, or else you would know that no youth so chosen to sup with the queen ever returns to his home again.'

'Yes,' said the prince, 'I am a stranger and have only come hither this day, and so do not understand these things. Even when I found you I was about to ask the way to some inn where folk of good condition lodge.'

'Then come home with me tonight,' said the old man. 'I live all alone, and I will tell you the trouble that lies upon this country.' Thereupon, taking the prince by the arm, he led him across the bridge and to another quarter of the town where he dwelt. He bade the servants prepare a fine supper, and he and the prince sat down to the table together. After they had made an end of eating and drinking, the old man told the prince all concerning those things of which he had spoken, and thus it was:

'When the king of this land died he left behind him three daughters—the most beautiful princesses in all of the world.

'Folk hardly dared speak of the eldest of them, but whisperings said that she was a sorceress, and that strange and gruesome things were done by her. The second princess was also a witch, though it was not said that she was evil, like the other. As for the youngest of the three, she was as beautiful as the morning and as gentle as a dove. When she was born a golden thread was about her neck, and it was foretold of her that she was to be the queen of that land.

'But not long after the old king died, the youngest princess vanished—no one could tell whither, and no one dared to ask—and the eldest princess had herself crowned as queen, and no one dared gainsay her. For a while everything went well enough, but by and by evil days came upon the land. Once every seven days the queen would bid some youth, young and strong, to sup with her, and from that time no one ever heard of him again, and no one dared ask what had become of him. At first it was the great folk at the queen's palace—officers and courtiers—who suffered; but by and by the sons of the merchants and the chief men of the city began to be taken. One time,' said the old man, 'I myself had three sons—as noble young men as could be found in the wide world. One day the chief of the queen's officers came to my house and asked me concerning how many sons I had. I was forced to tell him, and in a little while they were taken one by one to the queen's palace, and I never saw them again.

'But misfortune, like death, comes upon the young as well as the old. You yourself have had trouble, or else I am mistaken. Tell me what lies upon your heart, my son, for the talking of it makes the burthen lighter.'

The prince did as the old man bade him, and told all of his story; and so they sat talking and talking until far into the night, and the old man grew fonder and fonder of the prince the more he saw of him. So the end of the matter was that he asked the prince to live with him as his son, seeing that the young man had now no father and he no children, and the prince consented gladly enough.

So the two lived together like father and son, and the good old man began to take some joy in life once more.

But one day who should come riding up to the door but

the chief of the queen's officers.

'How is this?' said he to the old man, when he saw the prince. 'Did you not tell me that you had but three sons, and is this not a fourth?'

It was of no use for the old man to tell the officer that the youth was not his son, but was a prince who had come to visit that country. The officer drew forth his tablets and wrote something upon them, and then went his way, leaving the old man sighing and groaning. 'Ah, me!' said he, 'my heart sadly forebodes trouble.'

Sure enough, before three days had passed a bidding came to the prince to make ready to sup with the queen that night.

When evening drew near a troop of horsemen came, bringing a white horse with a saddle and bridle of gold studded with precious stones, to take the prince to the queen's palace.

As soon as they had brought him thither, they led the prince to a room where was a golden table spread with a snow-white cloth and set with dishes of gold. At the end of the table the queen sat waiting for him, and her face was hidden by a veil of silver gauze. She raised the veil and looked at the prince, and when he saw her face he stood as one wonderstruck, for not only was she so beautiful, but she set a spell upon him with the evil charm of her eyes. No one sat at the table but the queen and the prince, and a score of young pages served them, and sweet music sounded from a curtained gallery.

At last came midnight, and suddenly a great gong sounded from the courtyard outside. Then in an instant the music was stopped, the pages that served them hurried from the room, and presently all was as still as death.

Then, when all were gone, the queen arose and beckoned the prince, and he had no choice but to arise also and follow whither she led. She took him through the palace, where all was as still as the grave, and so came out by a postern door into a garden. Beside the postern a torch burned in a bracket. The queen took it down, and then led the prince up a path and under the silent trees until they came to a great wall of rough stone. She pressed her hand upon one of the great stones, and it opened like a door, and there was a flight of steps that led downward. The queen descended these steps, and the prince followed closely behind her. At the bottom was a long passageway, and at the farther end the prince saw what looked like a bright spark of light, as though the sun were shining. She thrust the torch into another bracket in the wall of the passage, and then led the way towards the light. It grew larger and larger as they went forward, until at last they came out at the farther end, and there the prince found himself standing in the sunlight and not far from the sea shore. The queen led the way towards the shore, when suddenly a great number of black dogs came running towards them, barking and snapping, and showing their teeth as though they would tear the two in pieces. But the queen drew from her bosom a whip with a steel-pointed lash, and as the dogs came springing towards them she laid about her right and left, till the skin flew and the blood ran, and the dogs leaped away howling and yelping.

At the edge of the water was a great stone mill, and the queen pointed towards it and bade the prince turn it. Strong as he was, it was as much as he could do to work it; but grind it he did, though the sweat ran down his face in streams. By and by a speck appeared far away upon the water; and as the prince ground and ground at the mill the speck grew larger and larger. It was something upon the water, and it came nearer and nearer as swiftly as the wind. At last it came close enough for him to see that it was a little boat all of brass. By and by the boat struck upon the beach, and as soon as it did so the queen entered it, bidding the prince do the same.

No sooner were they seated than away the boat went, still

as swiftly as the wind. On it flew and on it flew, until at last they came to another shore, the like of which the prince had never seen in his life before. Down to the edge of the water ran a garden—but such a garden! The leaves of the trees were all of silver and the fruit of gold, and instead of flowers were precious stones—white, red, yellow, blue and green—that flashed like sparks of sunlight as the breeze moved them this way and that way. Beyond the silver trees, with their golden fruit, was a great palace as white as snow, and so bright that one had to shut one's eyes as one looked upon it.

The boat ran up on the beach close to just such a stone mill as the prince had seen upon the other side of the water, and then he and the queen stepped ashore. As soon as they had done so the brazen boat floated swiftly away, and in a little while was gone.

'Here our journey ends,' said the queen. 'Is it not a wonderful land, and well worth the seeing? Look at all these jewels and this gold, as plenty as fruits and flowers at home. You may take what you please; but while you are gathering them I have another matter after which I must look. Wait for me here, and by and by I will be back again.'

So saying, she turned and left the prince, going towards the castle back of the trees.

But the prince was a prince, and not a common man; he cared nothing for gold and jewels. What he did care for was to see where the queen went, and why she had brought him to this strange land. So, as soon as she had fairly gone, he followed after.

He went along under the gold and silver trees, in the direction she had taken, until at last he came to a tall flight of steps that led up to the doorway of the snow-white palace. The door stood open, and into it the prince went. He saw not a soul, but he heard a noise as of blows and the sound as of someone weeping. He followed the sound, until by and by he came to a great vaulted room in the very centre of the palace. A curtain hung at the doorway. The prince lifted it and peeped within, and this was what he saw:

In the middle of the room was a marble basin of water as clear as crystal, and around the sides of the basin were these words, written in letters of gold:

'Whatsoever is False, that I make True.'

Beside the fountain upon a marblestand stood a statue of a beautiful woman made of alabaster, and around the neck of the statue was a thread of gold. The queen stood beside the statue, and beat and beat it with her steel-tipped whip. And all the while she lashed it the statue sighed and groaned like a living being, and the tears ran down its stone cheeks as though it were a suffering Christian. By and by the queen rested for a moment, and said, panting, 'Will you give me the thread of gold?' and the statue answered 'No.' Whereupon she fell to raining blows upon it as she had done before.

So she continued, now beating the statue and now asking it whether it would give her the thread of gold, to which the statue always answered 'No,' and all the while the prince stood gazing and wondering. By and by the queen wearied of what she was doing, and thrust the steel-tipped lash back into her bosom again, upon which the prince, seeing that she was done, hurried back to the garden where she had left him and pretended to be gathering the golden fruit and jewel flowers.

The queen said nothing to him good or bad, except to command him to grind at the great stone mill as he had done on the other side of the water. Thereupon the prince did as she bade, and presently the brazen boat came skimming over the water more swiftly than the wind. Again the queen and the prince entered it, and again it carried them to the other side whence they had come.

No sooner had the queen set foot upon the shore than she stopped and gathered up a handful of sand. Then, turning as quick as lightning, she flung it into the prince's face. 'Be a black dog,' she cried in a loud voice, 'and join your comrades!'

And now it was that the ring that the prince's mother had given him stood him in good stead. But for it he would have become a black dog like those others, for thus it had happened to all before him who had ferried the witch queen over the water. So she expected to see him run away yelping, as those others had done; but the prince remained a prince, and stood looking her in the face.

When the queen saw that her magic had failed her she grew as pale as death, and fell to trembling in every limb. She turned and hastened quickly away, and the prince followed her wondering, for he neither knew the mischief she had intended doing him, nor how his ring had saved him from the fate of those others.

So they came back up the stairs and out through the stone wall into the palace garden. The queen pressed her hand against the stone and it turned back into its place again. Then, beckoning to the prince, she hurried away down the garden. Before he followed he picked up a coal that lay near by, and put a cross upon the stone; then he hurried after her, and so came to the palace once more.

By this time the cocks were crowing, and the dawn of day was just beginning to show over the rooftops and the chimney stacks of the town.

As for the queen, she had regained her composure, and, bidding the prince wait for her a moment, she hastened to her chamber. There she opened her book of magic, and in it she soon found who the prince was and how the ring had saved him.

When she had learned all that she wanted to know she put on a smiling face and came back to him. 'Ah, prince,' said she,

'I well know who you are, for your coming to my country is not secret to me. I have shown you strange things tonight. I will unfold all the wonder to you another time. Will you not come back and sup with me again?'

'Yes,' said the prince, 'I will come whensoever you bid me;' for he was curious to know the secret of the statue and the strange things he had seen.

'And will you not give me a pledge of your coming?' said the queen, still smiling.

'What pledge shall I give you,' said the prince.

'Give me the ring that is upon your finger,' said the queen; and she smiled so bewitchingly that the prince could not have refused her had he desired to do so.

Alas for him! He thought no evil, but, without a word, drew off the ring and gave it to the queen, and she slipped it upon her finger.

'O fool!' she cried, laughing a wicked laugh, 'O fool! To give away that in which your safety lay!' As she spoke she dipped her fingers into a basin of water that stood near by and dashed the drops into the prince's face. 'Be a raven,' she cried, 'and a raven remain!'

In an instant the prince was a prince no longer, but a coal-black raven. The queen snatched up a sword that lay near by and struck at him to kill him. But the raven prince leaped aside and the blow missed its aim.

By good luck a window stood open, and before the queen could strike again he spread his wings and flew out of the open casement and over the housetops and was gone.

On he flew and on he flew until he came to the old man's house, and so to the room where his foster father himself was sitting. He lit upon the ground at the old man's feet and tried to tell him what had befallen, but all that he could say was 'Croak! Croak!'

'What brings this bird of ill omen?' said the old man, and he drew his sword to kill it. He raised his hand to strike, but the raven did not try to fly away as he had expected, but bowed his neck to receive the stroke. Then the old man saw that the tears were running down from the raven's eyes, and he held his hand. 'What strange thing is this?' he said. 'Surely nothing but the living soul weeps; and how, then, can this bird shed tears?' So he took the raven up and looked into his eyes, and in them he saw the prince's soul. 'Alas!' he cried, 'my heart misgives me that something strange has happened. Tell me, is this not my foster son, the prince?'

The raven answered 'Croak!' and nothing else; but the good old man understood it all, and the tears ran down his cheeks and trickled over his beard. 'Whether man or raven, you shall still be my son,' said he, and he held the raven close in his arms and caressed it.

He had a golden cage made for the bird, and every day he would walk with it in the garden, talking to it as a father talks to his son.

One day when they were thus in the garden together a strange lady came towards them down the pathway. Over her hat and face was drawn a thick veil, so that the two could not tell who she was. When she came close to them she raised the veil, and the raven prince saw that her face was the living likeness of the queen's; and yet there was something in it that was different. It was the second sister of the queen, and the old man knew her and bowed before her.

'Listen,' said she. 'I know what the raven is, and that it is the prince, whom the queen has bewitched. I also know nearly as much of magic as she, and it is that alone that has saved me so long from ill. But danger hangs close over me; the queen only waits for the chance to bewitch me; and some day she will overpower me, for she is stronger than I. With the prince's aid I can overcome her and make myself forever safe, and it is this that has brought me here today. My magic is powerful enough to change the prince back into his true shape again, and I will do so if he will aid me in what follows, and this is it: I will conjure the queen, and by and by a great eagle will come flying, and its plumage will be as black as night. Then I myself will become an eagle, with black-and-white plumage, and we two will fight in the air. After a while we will both fall to the ground, and then the prince must cut off the head of the black eagle with a knife I shall give him. Will you do this?' said she, turning to the raven, 'if I transform you to your true shape?'

The raven bowed his head and said 'Croak!' And the sister of the queen knew that he meant yes.

Therewith she drew a great, long, keen knife from her bosom, and thrust it into the ground. 'It is with this knife of magic,' said she, 'that you must cut off the black eagle's head.' Then the witch princess gathered up some sand in her hand, and flung it into the raven's face. 'Resume,' cried she, 'your own shape!' And in an instant the prince was himself again. The next thing the sister of the queen did was to draw a circle upon the ground around the prince, the old man, and herself. On the circle she marked strange figures here and there. Then, all three standing close together, she began her conjurations, uttering strange words—now under her breath, and now clear and loud.

Presently the sky darkened, and it began to thunder and rumble. Darker it grew and darker, and the thunder crashed and roared. The earth trembled under their feet, and the trees swayed hither and thither as though tossed by a tempest. Then suddenly the uproar ceased and all grew as still as death, the clouds rolled away, and in a moment the sun shone out once more, and all was calm and serene as it had been before. But still the princess muttered her conjurations, and as the prince and the old man looked, they beheld a speck that grew larger and larger, until they saw that it was an eagle as black as night that was coming swiftly flying through the sky. Then the queen's sister also saw it and ceased from her spells. She drew a little cap of feathers from her bosom with trembling hands. 'Remember,' said she to the prince; and, so saying, clapped the feather cap upon her head. In an instant she herself became an eagle—pied, black and white—and, spreading her wings, leaped into the air.

For a while the two eagles circled around and around; but at last they dashed against one another, and, grappling with their talons, tumbled over and over until they struck the ground close to the two who stood looking.

Then the prince snatched the knife from the ground and ran to where they lay struggling. 'Which was I to kill?' said he to the old man.

'Are they not birds of a feather?' cried the foster father. 'Kill them both, for then only shall we all be safe.'

The prince needed no second telling to see the wisdom of what the old man said. In an instant he struck off the heads of both the eagles, and thus put an end to both sorceresses, the lesser as well as the greater. They buried both of the eagles in the garden without telling any one of what had happened. So soon as that was done the old man bade the prince tell him all that had befallen him, and the prince did so.

'Aye! aye!' said the old man, 'I see it all as clear as day. The black dogs are the young men who have supped with the queen, the statue is the good princess, and the basin of water is the water of life, which has the power of taking away magic. Come, let us make haste to bring help to all those unfortunates who have been lying under the queen's spells.'

The prince needed no urging to do that. They hurried to the palace; they crossed the garden to the stone wall. There they found the stone upon which the prince had set the black cross. He pressed his hand upon it, and it opened to him like a door.

They descended the steps, and went through the passageway, until they came out upon the sea shore. The black dogs came leaping towards them; but this time it was to fawn upon them, and to lick their hands and faces.

The prince turned the great stone mill till the brazen boat came flying towards the shore. They entered it, and so crossed the water and came to the other side. They did not tarry in the garden, but went straight to the snow-white palace and to the great vaulted chamber where was the statue. 'Yes,' said the old man, 'it is the youngest princess, sure enough.'

The prince said nothing, but he dipped up some of the water in his palm and dashed it upon the statue. 'If you are the princess, take your true shape again,' said he. Before the words had left his lips the statue became flesh and blood, and the princess stepped down from where she stood, and the prince thought that he had never seen any one so beautiful as she. 'You have brought me back to life,' said she, 'and whatever I shall have shall be yours as well as mine.'

Then they all set their faces homeward again, and the prince took with him a cupful of the water of life.

When they reached the farther shore the black dogs came running to meet them. The prince sprinkled the water he carried upon them, and as soon as it touched them that instant they were black dogs no longer, but the tall, noble young men that the sorceress queen had bewitched. There, as the old man had hoped, he found his own three sons, and kissed them with the tears running down his face.

But when the people of that land learned that their youngest princess, and the one whom they loved, had come back again, and that the two sorceresses would trouble them no longer, they shouted and shouted for joy. All the town was hung with flags and illuminated, the fountains ran with wine, and nothing was heard but sounds of rejoicing. In the midst of it all the prince married the princess, and so became the king of that country.

And now to go back again to the beginning.

After the youngest prince had been driven away from home, and the old king had divided the kingdom betwixt the other two, things went for a while smoothly and joyfully. But by little and little the king was put to one side until he became as nothing in his own land. At last, hot words passed between the father and the two sons, and the end of the matter was that the king was driven from the land to shift for himself.

Now, after the youngest prince had married and had become king of that other land, he bethought himself of his father and his mother, and longed to see them again. So he set forth and travelled towards his old home. In his journeying he came to a lonely house at the edge of a great forest, and there night came upon him. He sent one of the many of those who rode with him to ask whether he could not find lodging there for the time, and who should answer the summons but the king, his father, dressed in the coarse clothing of a forester. The old king did not know his own son in the kingly young king who sat upon his snow-white horse. He bade the visitor to enter, and he and the old queen served their son and bowed before him.

The next morning the young king rode back to his own land, and then sent attendants with horses and splendid clothes, and bade them bring his father and mother to his own home.

He had a noble feast set for them, with everything befitting the entertainment of a king, but he ordered that not a grain of salt should season it.

So the father and the mother sat down to the feast with their son and his queen, but all the time they did not know him. The old king tasted the food and tasted the food, but he could not eat of it.

'Do you not feel hungry?' said the young king.

'Alas,' said his father, 'I crave your majesty's pardon, but there is no salt in the food.'

'And so is life lacking of savor without love,' said the young king; 'and yet because I loved you as salt you disowned me and cast me out into the world.'

Therewith he could contain himself no longer, but with the tears running down his cheeks kissed his father and his mother; and they knew him, and kissed him again.

Afterwards the young king went with a great army into the country of his elder brothers, and, overcoming them, set his father upon his throne again. If ever the two got back their crowns you may be sure that they wore them more modestly than they did the first time.

12

WOMAN'S WIT

When man's strength fails, woman's wit prevails.

In the days when the great and wise King Solomon lived and ruled, evil spirits and demons were as plentiful in the world as wasps in summer.

So King Solomon, who was so wise and knew so many potent spells that he had power over evil such as no man has had before or since, set himself to work to put those enemies of mankind out of the way. Some he conjured into bottles, and sank into the depths of the sea; some he buried in the earth; some he destroyed altogether, as one burns hair in a candle flame.

Now, one pleasant day when King Solomon was walking in his garden with his hands behind his back, and his thoughts busy as bees with this or that, he came face to face with a demon, who was a prince of his kind. 'Ho, little man!' cried the evil spirit, in a loud voice, 'art not thou the wise King Solomon who conjures my brethren into brass chests and glass bottles? Come, try a fall at wrestling with me, and whoever conquers shall be master over the other for all time. What do you say to such an offer as that?'

'I say aye!' said King Solomon, and, without another word,

he stripped off his royal robes and stood bare breasted, man to man with the other.

The world never saw the like of that wrestling match betwixt the king and the demon, for they struggled and strove together from the seventh hour in the morning to the sunset in the evening, and during that time the sky was clouded over as black as night, and the lightning forked and shot, and the thunder roared and bellowed, and the earth shook and quaked.

But at last the king gave the enemy an under twist, and flung him down on the earth so hard that the apples fell from the trees; and then, panting and straining, he held the evil one down, knee on neck. Thereupon the sky presently cleared again, and all was as pleasant as a spring day.

King Solomon bound the demon with spells, and made him serve him for seven years. First, he had him build a splendid palace, the like of which was not to be seen within the bounds of the seven rivers; then he made him set around the palace a garden, such as I for one wish I may see some time or other. Then, when the demon had done all that the king wished, the king conjured him into a bottle, corked it tightly, and set the royal seal on the stopper. Then he took the bottle a thousand miles away into the wilderness, and, when no man was looking, buried it in the ground, and this is the way the story begins.

Well, the years came and the years went, and the world grew older and older, and kept changing (as all things do but two), so that by and by the wilderness where King Solomon had hid the bottle became a great town, with people coming and going, and all as busy as bees about their own business and other folks' affairs.

Among these townspeople was a little tailor, who made clothes for many a worse man to wear, and who lived all alone in a little house with no one to darn his stockings for him, and no one to meddle with his coming and going, for he was a bachelor.

The little tailor was a thrifty soul, and by hook and crook had laid by enough money to fill a small pot, and then he had to bethink himself of some safe place to hide it. So one night he took a spade and a lamp and went out in the garden to bury his money. He drove his spade into the ground—and click! He struck something hard that rang under his foot with a sound as of iron. 'Hello!' said he, 'what have we here?' and if he had known as much as you and I do, he would have filled in the earth, and tramped it down, and have left that plate of broth for somebody else to burn his mouth with.

As it was, he scraped away the soil, and then he found a box of adamant, with a ring in the lid to lift it by. The tailor clutched the ring and bent his back, and up came the box with the damp earth sticking to it. He cleaned the mould away, and there he saw, written in red letters, these words:

'Open not.'

You may be sure that after he had read these words he was not long in breaking open the lid of the box with his spade.

Inside the first box he found a second, and upon it the same words:

'Open not.'

Within the second box was another, and within that still another, until there were seven in all, and on each was written the same words:

'Open not.'

Inside the seventh box was a roll of linen, and inside that a bottle filled with nothing but blue smoke; and I wish that bottle had burned the tailor's fingers when he touched it.

'And is this all?' said the little tailor, turning the bottle upside down and shaking it, and peeping at it by the light of the lamp. 'Well, since I have gone so far I might as well open it, as I have already opened the seven boxes.' Thereupon he broke the seal that stoppered it.

Pop! Out flew the cork, and—puff! out came the smoke; not all at once, but in a long thread that rose up as high as the stars, and then spread until it hid their light.

The tailor stared and goggled and gaped to see so much smoke come out of such a little bottle, and, as he goggled and stared, the smoke began to gather together again, thicker and thicker, and darker and darker, until it was as black as ink. Then out from it there stepped one with eyes that shone like sparks of fire, and who had a countenance so terrible that the tailor's skin quivered and shrivelled, and his tongue clove to the roof of his mouth at the sight of it.

'Who are thou?' said the terrible being, in a voice that made the very marrow of the poor tailor's bones turn soft from terror.

'If you please, sir,' said he, 'I am only a little tailor.'

The evil being lifted up both hands and eyes. 'How wonderful,' he cried, 'that one little tailor can undo in a moment that which took the wise Solomon a whole day to accomplish, and in the doing of which he wellnigh broke the sinews of his heart!' Then, turning to the tailor, who stood trembling like a rabbit, 'Hark thee!' said he. 'For two thousand years I lay there in that bottle, and no one came nigh to aid me. Thou hast liberated me, and thou shalt not go unrewarded. Every morning at the seventh hour I will come to thee, and I will perform for thee whatever task thou mayst command me. But there is one condition attached to the agreement, and woe be to thee if that condition is broken. If any morning I should come to thee, and thou hast no task for me to do, I shall wring thy neck as thou mightest wring the neck of a sparrow.' Thereupon he was gone in an instant, leaving the little tailor half dead with terror.

Now it happened that the prime minister of that country

had left an order with the tailor for a suit of clothes, so the next morning, when the demon came, the little man set him to work on the bench, with his legs tucked up like a journey-man tailor. 'I want,' said he, 'such and such a suit of clothes.'

'You shall have them,' said the demon; and thereupon he began snipping in the air, and cutting most wonderful patterns of silks and satins out of nothing at all, and the little tailor sat and gaped and stared. Then the demon began to drive the needle like a spark of fire—the like was never seen in all the seven kingdoms, for the clothes seemed to make themselves.

At last, at the end of a little while, the demon stood up and brushed his hands. 'They are done,' said he, and thereupon he instantly vanished. But the tailor cared little for that, for upon the bench there lay such a suit of clothes of silk and satin stuff, sewed with threads of gold and silver and set with jewels, as the eyes of man never saw before; and the tailor packed them up and marched off with them himself to the prime minister.

The prime minister wore the clothes to court that very day, and before evening they were the talk of the town. All the world ran to the tailor and ordered clothes of him, and his fortune was made. Every day the demon created new suits of clothes out of nothing at all, so that the tailor grew as rich as a Jew, and held his head up in the world.

As time went along he laid heavier and heavier tasks upon the demon's back, and demanded of him more and more; but all the while the demon kept his own counsel, and said never a word.

One morning, as the tailor sat in his shop window taking the world easy—for he had little or nothing to do now—he heard a great hubbub in the street below, and when he looked down he saw that it was the king's daughter passing by. It was the first time that the tailor had seen her, and when he saw her his heart stood still within him, and then began fluttering like a little bird, for one so beautiful was not to be met with in the four corners of the world. Then she was gone.

All that day the little tailor could do nothing but sit and think of the princess, and the next morning when the demon came he was thinking of her still.

'What hast thou for me to do today?' said the demon, as he always said of a morning.

The little tailor was waiting for the question.

'I would like you,' said he, 'to send to the king's palace, and to ask him to let me have his daughter for my wife.'

'Thou shalt have thy desire,' said the demon. Thereupon he smote his hands together like a clap of thunder, and instantly the walls of the room clove asunder, and there came out four-and-twenty handsome youths, clad in cloth of gold and silver. After these four-and-twenty there came another one who was the chief of them all, and before whom, splendid as they were, the four-and-twenty paled like stars in daylight. 'Go to the king's palace,' said the demon to that one, 'and deliver this message: The Tailor of Tailors, the Master of Masters, and One Greater than a King asks for his daughter to wife.'

'To hear is to obey,' said the other, and bowed his forehead to the earth.

Never was there such a hubbub in the town as when those five-and-twenty, in their clothes of silver and gold, rode through the streets to the king's palace. As they came near, the gates of the palace flew open before them, and the king himself came out to meet them. The leader of the five-and-twenty leaped from his horse, and, kissing the ground before the king, delivered his message: 'The Tailor of Tailors, the Master of Masters, and One Greater than a King asks for thy daughter to wife.'

When the king heard what the messenger said, he thought and pondered a long time. At last he said, 'If he who sent you is the Master of Masters, and greater than a king, let him send me an asking gift such as no king could send.'

'It shall be as you desire,' said the messenger, and thereupon the five-and-twenty rode away as they had come, followed by crowds of people.

The next morning when the demon came the tailor was ready and waiting for him. 'What hast thou for me to do to-day?' said the Evil One.

'I want,' said the tailor, 'a gift to send to the king such as no other king could send him.'

'Thou shalt have thy desire,' said the demon. Thereupon he smote his hands together, and summoned, not five-and-twenty young men, but fifty youths, all clad in clothes more splendid than the others.

All of the fifty sat upon coal-black horses, with saddles of silver and housings of silk and velvet embroidered with gold. In the midst of all the five-and-seventy there rode a youth in cloth of silver embroidered in pearls. In his hand he bore something wrapped in a white napkin, and that was the present for the king such as no other king could give. So said the demon: 'Take it to the royal palace, and tell his majesty that it is from the Tailor of Tailors, the Master of Masters, and One Greater than a King.'

'To hear is to obey,' said the young man, and then they all rode away.

When they came to the palace the gates flew open before them, and the king came out to meet them. The young man who bore the present dismounted and prostrated himself in the dust, and, when the king bade him arise, he unwrapped the napkin, and gave to the king a goblet made of one single ruby, and filled to the brim with pieces of gold. Moreover, the cup was of such a kind that whenever it was emptied of its money it instantly became full again. 'The Tailor of Tailors, the Master of Masters, and One Greater than a King sends your majesty this goblet, and bids me, his ambassador, to ask for your daughter,' said the young man.

When the king saw what had been sent him he was filled with amazement. 'Surely,' said he to himself, 'there can be no end to the power of one who can give such a gift as this.' Then to the messenger, 'Tell your master that he shall have my daughter for his wife if he will build over yonder a palace such as no man ever saw or no king ever lived in before.'

'It shall be done,' said the young man, and then they all went away, as the others had done the day before.

The next morning when the demon appeared, the tailor was ready for him. 'Build me,' said he, 'such and such a palace in such and such a place.'

And the demon said, 'It shall be done.' He smote his hands together, and instantly there came a cloud of mist that covered and hid the spot where the palace was to be built. Out from the cloud there came such a banging and hammering and clapping and clattering as the people of that town never heard before. Then when evening had come the cloud arose, and there, where the king had pointed out, stood a splendid palace as white as snow, with roofs and domes of gold and silver. As the king stood looking and wondering at this sight, there came five hundred young men riding, and one in the midst of all who wore a golden crown on his head, and upon his body a long robe stiff with diamonds and pearls. 'We come,' said he, 'from the Tailor of Tailors, and Master of Masters, and One Greater than a King, to ask you to let him have your daughter for his wife.'

'Tell him to come!' cried the king, in admiration, 'for the princess is his.'

The next morning when the demon came he found the tailor dancing and shouting for joy. 'The princess is mine!' he cried, 'so make me ready for her.'

'It shall be done,' said the demon, and thereupon he began to make the tailor ready for his wedding. He brought him to a marble bath of water, in which he washed away all that was coarse and ugly, and from which the little man came forth as beautiful as the sun. Then the demon clad him in the finest linen, and covered him with clothes such as even the emperor of India never wore. Then he smote his hands together, and the wall of the tailor's shop opened as it had done twice before, and there came forth forty slaves clad in crimson, and bearing bowls full of money in their hands. After them came two leading a horse as white as snow, with a saddle of gold studded with diamonds and rubies and emeralds and sapphires. After came a bodyguard of twenty warriors clad in gold armor. Then the tailor mounted his horse and rode away to the king's palace, and as he rode the slaves scattered the money amongst the crowd, who scrambled for it and cheered the tailor to the skies.

That night the princess and the tailor were married, and all the town was lit with bonfires and fireworks. The two rode away in the midst of a great crowd of nobles and courtiers to the palace which the demon had built for the tailor; and, as the princess gazed upon him, she thought that she had never beheld so noble and handsome a man as her husband. So she and the tailor were the happiest couple in the world.

But the next morning the demon appeared as he had appeared ever since the tailor had let him out of the bottle, only now he grinned till his teeth shone and his face turned black. 'What hast thou for me to do?' said he, and at the words the tailor's heart began to quake, for he remembered what was to happen to him when he could find the demon no more work to do—that his neck was to be wrung—and now he began to see that he had all that he could ask for in the world. Yes; what was there to ask for now?

'I have nothing more for you to do,' said he to the demon;

'you have done all that man could ask—you may go now.'

'Go!' cried the demon, 'I shall not go until I have done all that I have to do. Give me work, or I shall wring your neck.' And his fingers began to twitch.

Then the tailor began to see into what a net he had fallen. He began to tremble like one in an ague. He turned his eyes up and down, for he did not know where to look for aid. Suddenly, as he looked out of the window, a thought struck him. 'Maybe,' thought he, 'I can give the demon such a task that even he cannot do it. Yes, yes!' he cried, 'I have thought of something for you to do. Make me out yonder in front of my palace a lake of water a mile long and a mile wide, and let it be lined throughout with white marble, and filled with water as clear as crystal.'

'It shall be done,' said the demon. As he spoke he spat in the air, and instantly a thick fog arose from the earth and hid everything from sight. Then presently from the midst of the fog there came a great noise of chipping and hammering, of digging and delving, of rushing and gurgling. All day the noise and the fog continued, and then at sunset the one ceased and the other cleared away. The poor tailor looked out the window, and when he saw what he saw his teeth chattered in his head, for there was a lake a mile long and a mile broad, lined within with white marble, and filled with water as clear as crystal, and he knew that the demon would come the next morning for another task to do.

That night he slept little or none, and when the seventh hour of the morning came the castle began to rock and tremble, and there stood the demon, and his hair bristled and his eyes shone like sparks of fire. 'What hast thou for me to do?' said he, and the poor tailor could do nothing but look at him with a face as white as dough.

'What hast thou for me to do?' said the demon again, and then at last the tailor found his wits and his tongue from sheer terror. 'Look!' said he, 'at the great mountain over yonder; remove it, and make in its place a level plain with fields and orchards and gardens.' And he thought to himself when he had spoken, 'Surely, even the demon cannot do that.'

'It shall be done,' said the demon, and, so saying, he stamped his heel upon the ground. Instantly the earth began to tremble and quake, and there came a great rumbling like the sound of thunder. A cloud of darkness gathered in the sky, until at last all was as black as the blackest midnight. Then came a roaring and a cracking and a crashing, such as man never heard before. All day it continued, until the time of the setting of the sun, when suddenly the uproar ceased, and the darkness cleared away; and when the tailor looked out of the window the mountain was gone, and in its place were fields and orchards and gardens.

It was very beautiful to see, but when the tailor beheld it his knees began to smite together, and the sweat ran down his face in streams. All that night he walked up and down and up and down, but he could not think of one other task for the demon to do.

When the next morning came the demon appeared like a whirlwind. His face was as black as ink and smoke, and sparks of fire flew from his nostrils.

'What have you for me to do?' cried he.

'I have nothing for you to do!' piped the poor tailor.

'Nothing?' cried the demon.

'Nothing.'

'Then prepare to die.'

'Stop!' cried the tailor, falling on his knees, 'let me first see my wife.'

'So be it,' said the demon, and if he had been wiser he would have said 'No.'

When the tailor came to the princess, he flung himself on his face, and began to weep and wail. The princess asked him what was the matter, and at last, by dint of question, got the story from him, piece by piece. When she had it all she began laughing. 'Why did you not come to me before?' said she, 'instead of making all this trouble and uproar for nothing at all? I will give the monster a task to do.' She plucked a single curling hair from her head. 'Here,' said she, 'let him take this hair and make it straight.'

The tailor was full of doubt; nevertheless, as there was nothing better to do, he took it to the demon.

'Hast thou found me a task to do?' cried the demon.

'Yes,' said the tailor. 'It is only a little thing. Here is a hair from my wife's head; take it and make it straight.'

When the demon heard what was the task that the tailor had set him to do he laughed aloud; but that was because he did not know. He took the hair and stroked it between his thumb and finger, and, when he was done, it curled more than ever. Then he looked serious, and slapped it between his palms, and that did not better matters, for it curled as much as ever. Then he frowned, and, began beating the hair with his palm upon his knees, and that only made it worse. All that day he labored and strove at his task trying to make that one little hair straight, and, when the sun set, there was the hair just as crooked as ever. Then, as the great round sun sank red behind the trees, the demon knew that he was beaten. 'I am conquered! I am conquered!' he howled, and flew away, bellowing so dreadfully that all the world trembled.

So ends the story, with only this to say:

Where man's strength fails, woman's wit prevails.

For, to my mind, the princess—not to speak of her husband the little tailor—did more with a single little hair and her mother wit than King Solomon with all his wisdom.

ABOUT TERRY O'BRIEN

Terry O'Brien is an academic with three decades of experience in teaching language and communication skills in India and abroad. He also headed a college under the auspices of the University of Delhi.

A prolific writer, with several books to his credit, Terry O'Brien is a reputed professional motivational speaker and a quizmaster.